NOW I HAVE A GUN

RED CLAW
PUBLISHING

. . .

First Edition, September 2016
Written by William S. Mitcham + Ellis Kross
Edited by Sidonie Laïller

ISBN: 978-0-9976453-2-3

Cover by Ellis Kross
Book Design by Ellis Kross

. . .

Now I Have A Gun

by
Ellis Kross
+
William S. Mitcham

Based on the Ellis Kross novel,
The March to Sundown

Revisions by
Sidonie Lailler

FADE IN:

INT. WEST HARLETON LIBRARY - NIGHT

At the table sits JAMES BACKER, 21, athletic, handsome like James Dean, open textbooks scattered all around him in no particular order. He lets out a sigh, drops his pen into the spine of his PSYCHOLOGY textbook, and rubs his baggy eyes before finally calling it a night.

EXT. WEST HARLETON CAMPUS - NIGHT

With his bookbag worn over his shoulder, James passes a bronze statue, DEAN COOKE, in the COURTYARD.

EXT. COLLEGE STREET - NIGHT

James strolls down the sidewalk. Approaches his apartment where a couple of cars are parked out front. Lights burning inside. James is dismayed from the sight of the party.

INT. JAMES'S TOWNHOUSE - NIGHT

James is greeted by a rowdy crowd playing a drinking game with James's "little" brother, ROB, 19, a scrawny burnout who lives in the shadow of James.

>   PARTYGOER (O.S.)
>   Speak of the devil...

>   ROB
>   Yo, big bro! Come have a drink!

James ignores Rob and storms upstairs.

>   ROB (CONT'D)
>   Hey, Jimmy! Where you going?

INT. KITCHEN, JAMES'S TOWNHOUSE - CONTINUOUS

Rob takes a swig of beer.

>   PARTYGOER #2
>   Dude, what's up with your brother?

ROB
(under his breath)
He's being a jackass. Like always.

Rob SLAMS the red UNO card on the table, laughs ping-pong all around the table.

ROB (CONT'D)
BOOM! You know what that
means! Drink up, my brohemian!

INT. JAMES'S BEDROOM - NIGHT

James tosses and turns in bed from the heavy commotion downstairs. He FLINGS the blanket aside. Rolls out of bed.

JAMES
(frustrated)
You gotta be fucking kidding me...

INT. KITCHEN, JAMES'S TOWNHOUSE - NIGHT

Rob and a couple others are pounding beers.

PARTYGOERS
Chug! Chug! Chug!

JAMES (O.S.)
Rob! Can I have a word with you?

Rob downs the rest of the beer, wipes his face.

JAMES (CONT'D)
Robert!

Rob staggers from his seat, then sashays his way to James.

EXT. PORCH, JAMES'S TOWNHOUSE - NIGHT

James crosses his arms, militant-like. He's pissed.

JAMES
Did it ever occur to you that I have
class tomorrow?

> ROB
> Jimmy, we're just blowing off some
> steam. Why you getting all mad?

> JAMES
> You don't get it. Do you? This is
> why Mom and Dad kicked your ass
> out to begin with --

INT. KITCHEN, JAMES'S TOWNHOUSE - CONTINUOUS

The PARTYGOERS giggle from the argument outside.

> ROB (O.S.)
> -- Please! What's a matter with you?
> I've been busting my ass all week
> looking for a job and this is the shit
> I get --

> PARTYGOER #3
> -- Here we go again.

EXT. PORCH, JAMES'S TOWNHOUSE - CONTINUOUS

James holds out his hands, now baffled by his little brother.

> JAMES
> Why do you do this all the time,
> Robert? You finally do something
> productive and you think that
> entitles you to get drunk!

Rob waves off the comment and gives him a "fuck you" glare.

> JAMES (CONT'D)
> You know what you're problem is?
> You're always thinking about
> yourself and you have absolutely no
> consideration for other people.
> None! Whatsoever --

> ROB
> -- You're such a fucking tightass.
> You know that?

                              JAMES
          Me? I'm the tightass? No, Robert!
          I'm the one with a job! I'm the one
          going to school! You're the one
          with nothing!

                              ROB
          <u>Fuck you</u>, Jimmy...

James grabs a light jacket and shoes from inside. Storms back outside. Past Rob.
Into the night.

EXT. STREETS, OLD TOWN - NIGHT

As the rain starts to fall, James passes a shady nightclub, DADDY'S
PLAYGROUND. A frail man SCREAMS from the alleyway! James curiously
checks out the noise, only to find a group of well-dressed men crowded next to a
dumpster near the back entrance of the nightclub.

EXT. ALLEYWAY, OLD TOWN - CONTINUOUS

A gunshot suddenly RINGS out!

From a distance, James witnesses HENRY FRICK, 32, being shot in the head.
James freezes, then turns to jello. He's spotted by one of the men. James takes
off running...

EXT. STREETS, OLD TOWN - CONTINUOUS

As James rounds the intersection, he's struck in the bridge of his nose by the butt
of a handgun. BAM! He falls to the ground and drifts in and out of
consciousness. Above James looms a strange, blurry thing -- a human-sized raven.

EXT. BRIDGE, OLD TOWN - NIGHT

The trunk of a Cadillac opens with a piercing SQUEAK. A bloody and beaten
James is pulled from the trunk. Then dragged to a railing where two others are
waiting in the downpour. Both individuals dressed like the night.

                      A MAN'S VOICE (O.S.)
          How much did he see?

                      ANOTHER MAN'S VOICE (O.S.)
          Everything.

                              JAMES
          Please...don't...I won't say anything -
          -

The SHOOTER pulls out a handgun from inside his coat and shoots James directly in the face!

INT. ROB'S BEDROOM, JAMES'S TOWNHOUSE - DAY

With a brutal hangover, Rob cracks open his bloodshot eyes. Then rolls out of the futon. Stretches away the ache.

INT. JAMES'S BEDROOM, JAMES'S TOWNHOUSE - DAY

Rob checks James's messy bed. Finds James's bookbag, as well as his baseball cleats, neatly positioned on the floor.

INT. JAMES'S TOWNHOUSE - DAY

Rob walks downstairs, tripping over an overturned chair along the way. He checks the KITCHEN. Beer cans are piled in the sink. He checks the LIVING ROOM. Empty as well.

EXT. PORCH, JAMES'S TOWNHOUSE - DAY

As Rob steps outside, a HELICOPTER lets out a guttural cough in the sky above! The sound of police SIRENS soon follow...

INT. LIVING ROOM, JAMES'S TOWNHOUSE - DAY

Concerned, Rob quickly flips through each channel until he comes across the LOCAL NEWS.

ON THE SCREEN

A young, blonde-haired REPORTER is reporting in front of a crime scene. Police scattered everywhere. Fire fighters are pulling the lifeless BODY of a male from the river.

EXT. BRIDGE, OLD TOWN - DAY

The paramedics are loading James into the helicopter. Rob pushes his way closer. COPS suddenly block his path...

> ROB
> That's my brother!

The cop tackles Rob. Other COPS rush to the cop's defense.

                              ROB (CONT'D)
          Lemme go! That's my fucking
          brother goddamn it!

The cops try to subdue Rob.

                              ROB (CONT'D)
              (crying)
          Jimmy! Jimmy! No...

INT. WAITING ROOM, HOSPITAL - DAY

Rob's mother, SUSANNAH, 55, short and feisty, and his father, THOMAS, 58, approach a shocked Rob. Rob stands to his feet. Breaks the news. Susannah breaks down after listening to James's prognosis. She cries into Rob's shoulder.

INT. HOSPITAL ROOM - NIGHT

James rests in a hospital bed -- a bandage wrapped around one half of his face while the other half is swollen and covered with cuts and bruises.

At James's bedside, Rob watches the NEWS REPORT on TV.

ON THE SCREEN

A young black man, CEDRIC GAINES, is being escorted from his rundown house by a group of COPS.

                              REPORTER (O.S.)
          Police have arrested twenty-three-
          year-old, Cedric Gaines, for the
          shooting of West Harleton student,
          James Backer. Backer currently
          remains in intensive care at
          Memorial Hospital.

BACK TO ROB

who scowls at the TV.

EXT. BRIDGE, OLD TOWN - NIGHT - DREAM (NIGHT OF THE SHOOTING)

Rain merrily TAPS through the BLACKNESS. The trunk door squeaks opens. Above towers a SHADOWY MAN...

INT. HOTEL ROOM, SEASIDE HEIGHTS - DAY - PRESENT DAY

Rob wakes up, rolls out of bed, and walks over to James's urn on the dresser. He walks to the BALCONY where he stares at the overcast sky above the Pacific Ocean.

INT. CYBER JAXX'S - DAY

In front of a computer, Rob scrolls through a Twitter page.

ON THE MONITOR

A tweet by @FlipperMan:

> "I be chillin' out at Holes with my
> 'crazee' crew at high noon."

Rob opens an Instagram page: a black and white photo of FLIP, 21, dressed like a model in a cologne advertisement, and WILT, somber demeanor, same age as Flip.

The comment below reads:

> "On the way 2 pic up Chemo."

BACK TO ROB

who writes down the word "HOLES" on a notepad. He places the notepad next to a six chambered REVOLVER inside his bookbag.

EXT. MAIN STREET, TOPSIDE - DAY

Across the street from Rob POLICE OFFICERS rope off the MAIN PIER with yellow caution tape.

INT. THE COVE - DAY

Rob slides into the booth and pulls out a "TRUCKER BY HEART" magazine from his bookbag.

The WAITRESS, an attractive woman who dresses as if she's rebelling against her own natural beauty, arrives at the table. Rob studies the metal studs and the fresh ink on her face as she hands him the menu.

>   ROB
>   (skimming the
>   menu)
>   How's the shrimp?

INT. MEN'S RESTROOM, THE COVE - DAY

Rob vomits in the toilet. Flushes. Then exits the stall. He washes his face with faucet water. Dries face with a towel from the dispenser. One of the stall doors suddenly SQUEAKS open, causing Rob to flinch!

In the mirror, Rob witnesses a STRANGE MAN, only his two legs and caramel-colored wingtips are visible below the stall...

>   LOCAL (O.S.)
>   Is everything all right?

Slack-faced, Rob turns to the LOCAL. Turns back to stall. No legs. No stranger. The stall is empty.

INT. THE COVE - DAY

The waitress makes one last stop at Rob's table.

>   WAITRESS
>   Was something wrong with the
>   food?

>   ROB
>   (clearing his throat)
>   No. It was fine.

>   WAITRESS
>   Would you like for me to box it up
>   for you?

As the waitress waits for a response, Rob's attention is drawn outside where Flip and Wilt cruise by in a black piece of shit HATCHBACK with its stereo bumping rap music.

EXT. HOLES, THE SQUARE - DAY

Rob approaches Flip's crazy crew: Wilt, CHEMO, 20's, lanky, bald-headed with a tattoo of a barcode on the back of his head, and SKETCH, 23, small in stature, as quiet as a mouse.

                              FLIP
                     (flicking head in a
                              nod)
                  What's good?

                              ROB
                  Sup. You know where I can score
                  some blow?

                              CHEMO
                  You a nark?

                              ROB
                  Nah, man. I ain't a nark. Are you?

Chemo's cheeks wash over red with anger.

                              CHEMO
                     (pointing at Rob)
                  Check out the fuckin' comedian --

                              FLIP
                  -- I may know a guy who knows a
                  guy, but from what I've heard, he
                  ain't gettin' straight till later tonight,
                  but if you're lookin' for some other
                  shit, I'd be more than happy to
                  hook you up.

INT. APPLE RIPPER'S HOUSE - DAY

Rob hands the cash to APPLE RIPPER, 30, scraggly beard, rail thin. In exchange,
he grabs a bag of WEED next to a homemade bowl made from an apple. Hands
the bag to Rob.

                              APPLE RIPPER
                  So, where you from, Cowboy?

                              ROB
                  Me? I'm from Philly.

                              APPLE RIPPER
                  No shit. Long way from home.

                              ROB
                  I'm on vacation.

Apple Ripper throws in a bag of mollies.

                              APPLE RIPPER
                  On that note, here's a little appetizer
                  for you. On the house.

INT. FLIP'S HATCHBACK - DAY

Flip blows a ring of smoke from his mouth, then hands the blunt to Rob, who takes bird-like hits. Rob coughs.

> FLIP
> (amusingly)
> You a'ight there, Philly.

> ROB
> Yeah. Good.

Red-eyed, Rob looks down at a corner of Chemo's wallet protruding from his back right pocket.

EXT. HOLES, THE SQUARE - DAY

Wilt swerves into the parking lot, tires screeching.

INT. FLIP'S HATCHBACK - DAY

Flip slaps hands with Rob.

> FLIP
> Thanks for the smokes, Philly.

> ROB
> No problemo. Thanks for the
> fucking chronic.

EXT. HOLES, THE SQUARE - DAY

Flip steps out with Rob. He pulls Rob aside, away from the other stoners waiting in the hatchback.

> FLIP
> So, what you gettin' into tonight,
> Philly Blunt?

> ROB
> Just gettin' straight with your boy.
> Right?

> FLIP
> A'ight then. You know where
> Grier's is at?

> ROB
> You mean the one off Shore
> Avenue?

                        FLIP
            That's the one, dawg. Meet me
            there at nine o'clock. A'ight?

                        ROB
            Yeah. A'ight.

EXT. SWEET TEE'S, TOPSIDE BOARDWALK - DAY

Rob digs through Chemo's wallet: a Trojan condom; a FREE SUB coupon.
Pockets the card. Cash as well. Lastly, he pulls out a pack of matches, which
reads "LEATHER N' LACE."

A QUICK FLASH of Rob sitting at the bar, watching ANTHONY FOSTER,
late 30's, a loud man with a loud appearance, in the front row, throwing dollar
bills at a cute STRIPPER.

Rob pockets the matches, then tosses the wallet in the trash.

EXT. TOPSIDE BOARDWALK - CONTINUOUS

Rob approaches a majestic band of CIRCUS FREAKS, including a snake-like man
named NILE, as well as a SWORDSWALLOWER and a WOLFMAN,
entertaining pedestrians. Rob stops. Watches.

EXT. THE AMAZING PRETZEL STAND, TOPSIDE BOARDWALK - DAY

A young server, JAZZ, 21, dresses the part of a teenager but she's able to pull it off,
drawing on a worn sketch pad. Rob makes his presence known by clearing his
throat.

                        JAZZ
            Can I help you?

                        ROB
            Best pretzels in town, huh?

Jazz shrugs, casually.

                        JAZZ
            Yep.

She removes herself from the drawing, looks at the sign next to the concession
stand.

                        JAZZ (CONT'D)
            Oh! Right. They're okay, I guess.

>   ROB
>   Uh, okay...
>   (furrowing his
>   brows)
>   ...I'll take cinnamon.

INT. ARCADE, GALATIA - DAY

The bright, flickering glow of "SPACE INVADERS" flashes over Rob's vacant face as he plays the popular arcade game.

INT. HOTEL ROOM, SEASIDE HEIGHTS - DAY

Rob anxiously checks the time on the TV's cable box. He turns to the closet. Walks over. Grabs the smut magazine, "BUSTIES," from his bookbag.

EXT. BACKER'S RESIDENCE - DAY

A black Lincoln pulls into the driveway of a two-story Charleston-style house. Decent neighborhood. Middle-class.

INT. BACKER'S RESIDENCE - DAY

Susannah guides seasoned DETECTIVE RUBY, 50's, stocky, scars on his face from teenage acne, to Rob's upstairs bedroom. Ruby stops before he reaches the room, notices the "height line" on the side of the doorway. Rob's LAST measurement stops at Ruby's chest level -- around five feet or so.

INT. ROB'S BEDROOM, BACKER'S RESIDENCE - CONTINUOUS

Susannah opens the door for Ruby. Music posters on the wall, lava lamp, stereo, computer, video games: typical room of a teenager. She waits at the doorway as Ruby examines Rob's personal belongings. He finds a chest next to Rob's bed.

>   SUSANNAH
>   Robert's the only one with the key.

>   RUBY
>   Do you mind?

>   SUSANNAH
>   Whatever it takes, John.

Ruby grabs a baseball trophy from the dresser and breaks off the lock. He opens the chest. His eyes light up in awe.

                                          RUBY
          Jesus.

INT. BATHROOM, HOTEL ROOM - CONTINUOUS

Rob splashes his face with water. Studies his pale face in the mirror. Notices a
dark stub on his right cheek. His eyebrows furrow with confusion.

A SQUEAK of a door!

INT. HOTEL ROOM, SEASIDE HEIGHTS - CONTINUOUS

Rob races from the bathroom. Walks to the cracked open door. Pokes out his
head. Nobody.

                              A MAN'S VOICE (O.S.)
                Miss me?

Startled, Rob spins around. Before him sits a debonair MOSES, 31, in the dark
corner of the room. He's wearing a silver suit. Legs crossed. Wingtip shoes.
Caramel-colored.

Moses leans forward into the dim light. His face disguised with a five o'clock
shadow; his hair gelled back.

                                          ROB
                  What are you doing here?

Moses stands and paces around the room.

                                        MOSES
                  Did you think you were going to
                  get rid of me that easily?

                                          ROB
                  I thought we agreed to go our
                  separate ways. That was the deal --

                                        MOSES
                  -- Deal? We never had a deal.

Rob takes a glance at the handle of the revolver protruding from his bookbag on
the dresser. Does a double-take.

                                          ROB
                  What the hell do you want?

Moses browses through one of Rob's smut magazines. Smirks.

                                        MOSES
                  I need to ask a favor.

                                          13

                               ROB
              You came all of this way to ask a
              favor?

A nod from Moses. Rob closes his eyes, then opens them. Moses is <u>still</u> there.
Waiting. Watching.

                        ROB (CONT'D)
             (unsteadily)
              How did you find me?

                       MOSES
              All I had to do was follow the
              breadcrumbs. If I can find you, he
              can find you. And he will...

Rob looks down at his shaky hands.

                       ROB
             A favor. That's all?

Again, a nod from Moses.

INT. BATHROOM, HOTEL ROOM - CONTINUOUS

Rob leans over the sink, hands shaking. He's crying, too.

                       ROB
             Shut up...
              (screaming)
             ...I said, 'Shut the fuck up!'

Rob punches the mirror, the glass breaks but never shatters completely. All that
remains is a spider web-like fracture.

INT. RED PINES - NIGHT

The ORDERLY escorts Ruby to Doctor Borough's office.

INT. DR. BOROUGH'S OFFICE, RED PINES - CONTINUOUS

Doctor WILLIAM BOROUGH, 47, salt and pepper hair, answers the door.
Ruby shakes the doctor's hand. Then displays a badge.

                              RUBY
                  John Ruby, private investigator. I
                  need to ask you a couple of
                  questions about one of your
                  patients. His name is Robert
                  Backer.

The doctor steps aside and points at his desk.

                              DR. BOROUGH
                  Yes, of course. Please have a seat,
                  Detective.

INT. BATHROOM, HOTEL ROOM - CONTINUOUS

Rob switches the timer to the heat lamp. He puts on a GOLD NECKLACE
with a pendant of a gold wing. Stares at his red fragmented reflection in the
broken mirror. Then dresses into a pair of clean clothes: a black v-neck sweater,
gray slacks, black wingtips. Lastly, he slides his left wrist into a ROLEX watch.

Once dressed, he pulls out the contents from his bookbag: the URN; the
REVOLVER; a SWITCHBLADE; two packs of MATCHES, one of them once
belonging to Chemo, the other belonging to Anthony Foster; a keychain holding a
RABBIT'S FOOT as well as a KEY; a rusty plate with the Volkswagen Beetle's
VIN number; then, a worn CASE holding a SYRINGE, SPOON, and BAND.

Lastly, he pulls out a Canon Rebel XTi CAMERA from his bookbag. Sets it
down on the sink as well. Rob holsters the revolver, as well as the blade. Then,
after he's equipped, he neatly places everything back inside his book bag, including
the urn.

INT. HOTEL ROOM, SEASIDE HEIGHTS - NIGHT

With a dime, Rob unscrews the panel to the AC panel and hides his bookbag
inside. Closes panel. Makes sure it's secured.

INT. THE LIQUOR STORE - NIGHT

Rob places a bottle of Jose Cuervo on top of the counter. Then he hands the
Haitian CLERK his driver's license. Rob grows paranoid as the clerk looks at the
license for a second too long.

INSERT - THE LICENSE, which reads:

                  "Henry Frick
                  2127 Wilkinson Court
                  Philadelphia, PA 19121"

BACK IN THE STORE

where the clerk stares at the ID, then hands it back to Rob.

INT. ROB'S HONDA CIVIC - NIGHT

Rob takes baby sips from the Cuervo while he smokes from a joint. A beam of headlights crosses the rear view mirror.

EXT. GRIER'S CONVENIENT STORE - CONTINUOUS

Flip pulls beside Rob's car. Rob rolls down the passenger window and lights up a cigarette. Flip, who's dressed the part, like a clubber, leans out the window, arm hanging outward, smoking as well. Music bumping.

> FLIP
> What's good, Philli Vanilli?

Without Flip paying attention, Rob carefully slides his hand over the passenger seat and grips the revolver.

> ROB
> Just chillin', man. So, what's the
> plan?

EXT. DREW'S HOUSE - NIGHT

Rob waits inside his car while Flip runs inside.

INT. ROB'S HONDA CIVIC - CONTINUOUS

Rob watches Flip and his "dude," DREW, a few years older than Flip, get inside Drew's used Toyota Camry. They drive off. Rob places the revolver inside the glove box. Follows Drew.

EXT./INT. CRYSTAL PALACE - NIGHT

The bouncer, ZEEK, about the size of a fridge, no neck, all muscle, slaps hands with Flip, who, in return, leans close and puts in a good word for the guest, Rob. Zeek admits both Drew and Rob after he pats down both of their pockets.

Lightning storms of strobe lights dance throughout the dimly lit club as dance music blasts like a barrage of gunfire.

Rob passes droves of gorgeous women lingering around an ice sculpture of a fountain while above a range of glaciers shaped like Egyptian pyramids plays VHS tapes of avant-garde style clips with chicly dressed women pleasuring themselves inside decrepit mansions from the eighteenth century.

Drew acknowledges an old pal and splits while Rob and Flip prowl down a hallway covered in a red, ominous light.

INT. DANCE FLOOR, CRYSTAL PALACE - CONTINUOUS

The hallway tiers downward into an amphitheatre-type room. The red light dissipates into a wall of soft blue light over a bobbing sea of flesh.

One side of the room consists of a lounging area overcast with a cloud of dense smoke. All of the furniture is high end stuff, too. A buffet of women. All shapes and sizes.

> FLIP
> Take your pick.

Amused, Rob smirks from the sight of the model-like women.

> ROB
> Not bad.

Next to the dance floor: a VIP section where greasy swingers are doing lines of coke off a young WOMAN'S stomach while she lies naked on top of a table. Rob cranes his head above Flip for a closer inspection. More women pleasuring themselves. Flickers of light bring out the orgy inside the VIP.

> ROB (CONT'D)
> Is your 'boy' here?

Flip checks his phone, then shakes his head.

> FLIP
> Nah. Not yet. He said he's 'on the
> way.' Don't worry, man. He'll be
> here shortly.

> ROB
> I'm gonna grab a drink.

Along the way to the bar, Rob scopes out the place. Two areas grab his attention: one, a RED DOOR with the sign "EMPLOYEES ONLY" and the other, a STAIRCASE next to the MAIN STAGE. Both areas are heavily guarded with SECURITY.

INT. BAR, CRYSTAL PALACE - CONTINUOUS

Rob orders a beer from the BARTENDER while a handsome, hollow-cheeked man in an expensive black suit with a black dress shirt and black tie approaches the bar. This is NICO WEST, 30's, a metrosexual brimming with an intoxicating confidence.

The bartender already has Nico's drink, a Tom Collins, waiting for him. Nico sips from drink, then faces Rob.

> NICO
> I've never seen you here before...

> ROB
> (hesitantly)
> First time.

> NICO
> Is that so?
> (raising glass in a
> toast)
> We're glad you came out, my
> friend.

Nico reaches out his other hand.

> ROB
> Name's ah Jimmy, but you can call
> me Philly.

> NICO
> Nicholas West, but you can call me
> Nico.

Rob keeps his cool by shaking Nico's hand.

> NICO (CONT'D)
> Pleasure to meet you, Philly.

The blue lights suddenly go red all around the club. The music intensifies as Rob cautiously eases his hand around his back, toward the switchblade tucked underneath his belt...

EXT. TOPSIDE BEACH - DAY

A SCREECH of a seagull cuts across the blue sky. Rob's bloodshot eyes open, then blink their way into consciousness. He sits upright and scans the beach with mild confusion.

Rob attempts to stand but a sharp pain in his head keeps him seated. He checks his clothes, which are the same as last night; however, sandy and wrinkled. Then, he pats down his pockets, like a cop. The switchblade is gone, too...

A QUICK FLASH of Drew weaving around clubbers, then purposefully bumping into Rob from behind, resulting in Rob dropping the switchblade from his grip.

Rob searches through the sand but comes up empty. A couple of footprints, smaller than Rob's foot, lead back to a walkway behind him. He pulls out a wadded tissue stained with blood. Cringes from the sight of a used condom inside.

A QUICK FLASH of Rob having sex with a blonde haired girl, JAMIE, 20's, as thin as a runway model, in an infinity pool.

Rob investigates the various imprints scattered around him.

QUICK FLASHES — MEMORIES OF ROB HAVING SEX

-- Rob slides his hand around Jamie's neck as he makes out with her. His hand moves over her breasts, caressing them.

-- A ravenous Jamie pushes Rob to the sand, straddles him.

-- Moaning with ecstasy, Jamie rides Rob on the beach.

Rob scratches his eyes, takes in a deep breath. Checks his red, crusty groin. Embraces yet another healthy breath.

As Rob shifts to his right side, he finds the Rolex digging into his side. He picks up the Rolex. Puts it on. The side of his arm is covered with bruises. Same with his knuckles.

EXT. NICO'S STREET - DAY

Rob makes it back to his Civic parked on the side of the road. Not too far is Nico's luxurious beach house...

EXT. MAIN STREET, TOPSIDE - DAY

Rob stops at the intersection before his motel. A police CRUISER is parked outside, forcing Rob to do a U-turn.

INT. PARKING GARAGE - CONTINUOUS

Rob locates a clear view of the motel. Steps out of car. Watches the two POLICE OFFICERS follow the MANAGER of Seaside Heights to Rob's room. They go inside without even knocking.

Rob goes to the nearest payphone. Then he dials 9-1-1.

> OPERATOR (V.O.)
> 911. Please state your emergency?

INT. ROB'S HONDA CIVIC - DAY

As Rob's about to exit the garage, the two officers receive the dispatch, then get inside the cruiser and drive away.

EXT. MAIN LOBBY, SEASIDE HEIGHTS - DAY

Rob waits for the manager to walk back to his OFFICE, then creeps underneath the window. On the TV above the desk clerk's counter: a rusty crane's hoisting a gray BEETLE from the heavily trafficked Los Angeles Canal.

ON THE SCREEN

A swarm of cruisers, as well as unmarked cars, are gathered around the junkyard, the crane's pulling the waterlogged Beetle above the head of a Barbie Doll-like REPORTER.

INT. HOTEL ROOM, SEASIDE HEIGHTS - DAY

Rob checks the AC unit first. Unscrews the panel. Grabs the bookbag from inside. Everything's still there. Check.

INT. BATHROOM, HOTEL ROOM - CONTINUOUS

Rob strips, washes his face in the sink, then dampens a paper towel and washes his armpits. Check.

As Rob's about to throw on some clothes, he touches scratch marks on his back. Long and red, the work of Freddy Krueger.

A QUICK FLASH of Rob on Topside Beach last night, Jamie digging her purple nails into Rob's back as he fucks her.

Rob closes his eyes, pinches the bridge of his nose. Then checks the cash in his bookbag. Counts only twelve dollars.

EXT. BEACH ACCESS PARKING, HERALD'S POINT - DAY

Rob parks the Civic. Grabs his things from the passenger seat, including the revolver from the glove box.

EXT./INT. FORECLOSED HOUSE - DAY

Rob sneaks around the back, peeking through each window along the way. He unlocks the back door with a trusty pick.

First, Rob checks the KITCHEN. Clear. Then, he checks the LIVING ROOM. Both rooms are tomb-empty. Rob walks past a holey sleeping bag, as well as candy wrappers on the floor. Checks the other rooms, including the a gutted BEDROOM across the hall. The closets. Empty.

From the KITCHEN, he gathers shards of broken glass in the sink. Pockets one of the shards and sprinkles the other pieces behind both the front and back door.

Lastly, he grabs a sturdy TWO BY FOUR from the closet.

INT. BATHROOM, FORECLOSED HOUSE - CONTINUOUS

Rob closes the broken door, then props the two by four underneath the door handle. Then he surveys the filthy room. Cockroaches scurry along the baseboards. Shit and cum stains splattered over the floor like a crime scene. A used condom floats in the clogged toilet like a life preserver. Another shriveled condom is attached to the wall like old spaghetti.

Suddenly, Rob lunges over the sink and vomits, mostly stomach bile. Turns on the faucet. Instead of water, he receives several angry spits of brown whatever.

Rob turns to a nasty bathtub, lies inside, then reaches inside his pocket and pulls out the revolver. Looks it over. Empties the bullets from the chamber. He inserts one while pocketing the rest. Spins the chamber. Closes the chamber.

Then, Rob involuntarily presses the barrel underneath his chin and squeezes the trigger...

CLICK!

Rob loosens his flexed face and cries. Niagara Falls.

EXT. BRIDGE, OLD TOWN - NIGHT - DREAM (NIGHT OF THE SHOOTING)

Rain BEATING all around Rob, over the asphalt, over his shoulders and face. He peers around and finds himself standing between the same two individuals from earlier. Their arms are clasped around his elbows.

In front of a swaying Rob stands Nico's father, CONRAD WEST, 50's, similar profile to Nico, older face, grayer hair. Conrad points the wet GLOCK directly at Rob's face.

>   CONRAD
>   When you meet God, ask Him to
>   forgive me...

A flash of lightning STREAKS like a vein in the black sky, then a deafening
BANG from above!

INT. BATHROOM, FORECLOSED HOUSE - DAY - PRESENT DAY

Rob bolts upright, his breath laborious. He looks around. Still hears the same
BEATING sound, but this time thinner. He staggers to the window where across
the street a ROOFER is nailing down a shingle on a roof. Rob checks the time.

EXT. KING STREET, OLD TOWN - DAY

Rob locates a dive at the end of a STRIP MALL called REUBEN'S RIBS where a
decent line of people is wrapped like garnish around the front of the smoking hut-
like structure.

EXT. REUBEN'S RIBS - DAY

Rob PURPOSEFULLY bumps shoulders with one of Reuben's CUSTOMERS
who shares the same attributes as a walrus.

>   ROB
>   (apologetically)
>   Sorry. Didn't see you.

INT. HEROES VS. VILLAINS COMICS - DAY

As Rob browses the aisles, he counts out sixty-four dollars inside the customer's
Velcro wallet. He strolls past a display case of vintage comic books, including
"THE AMAZING SPIDERMAN" #5 issue, which is locked up. No problem.

The SALESMAN, a long haired hipster who appears as if he follows daily hipster
trends, greets Rob with a half-smile.

>   SALESMAN
>   Ah! The Amazing Spiderman...
>   (pocketing his
>   hands)
>   ...A classic indeed.

Rob's eyes the salesman's keys worn around his neck.

INT. THE PAWNSHOP - DAY

Rob hands "THE AMAZING SPIDERMAN" comic to THE RUSSIAN, 40's, hunched shoulders, going bald by the minute, everything about his appearance is outdated and belongs in a museum.

                    THE RUSSIAN (O.S.)
          I'll give you five for it.

                    ROB
          Seven-fifty.

                    THE RUSSIAN
          Five hundred. Take it or leave.

The door opens with the DING of a cowbell. The girl from the pretzel stand walks as quiet as a breeze to the counter.

                    THE RUSSIAN (O.S.) (CONT'D)
          Is there a problem, my friend?

Rob snaps from his daze and faces the unfashionable Russian.

                    ROB
          Deal.

Rob shakes his meaty hand as Jazz approaches from behind.

                    JAZZ
          Hey, the pretzel guy...
                    (pointing at Rob)
          ...So, how was your pretzel?

                    ROB
          It was probably the best pretzel I've
          ever eaten.

                    JAZZ
          Really? That's what I've heard.

Rob nods at the vinyl player in her arms.

                    ROB
          A Conley, huh?

Jazz sets the vinyl player on the counter.

23

>   THE RUSSIAN
>   (butting in)
>   Good product, yeah?

Rob looks over Jazz, the embarrassment on her face.

>   ROB
>   Top of the line. A player like that
>   goes for at least three hundred on
>   the market, if you're lucky to find
>   one as cheap as that.

Jazz sneaks a glance at Rob. Then smiles.

>   ROB (CONT'D)
>   Name's Jimmy.

Rob extends his hand, which catches Jazz off guard.

>   JAZZ
>   (shaking Rob's hand)
>   Jazz.

INT. INTERNET CAFE, CYBER JAXX'S - DAY

Rob scrolls through the website, FINDER.

ON THE MONITOR

Jazz's birth name: Samantha Jasper Caldwell who resides in an apartment complex called Glendale Straits, APT.101, with her forty-four-year-old mother, PHYLLIS CALDWELL.

Rob checks Jazz's Twitter account. Her latest tweet reads:

>   "Drinking coffee while doodling
>   angels :)"

He clicks on a photo link attached to her tweet: a CLOSE UP of an angel. He pulls up her artwork, professionally done movie posters, one being "MAD MAX BEYOND THUNDERDOME."

He closes her Twitter page, opens her Facebook page, and searches through her photo albums, mostly Polaroids taken with a burly fellow with the hashtag "Throwback Thursday."

Then, finally, he opens a selfie of Jazz: she's posing for the mirror in a skimpy lime green dress -- a see-through dress, depending from the angle on the monitor.

Below the photo reads:

"Posted eight days ago."

BACK TO ROB

who opens Flip's Instagram page. Checks out latest photo.

ON THE MONITOR

Moses is standing among a group of clubbers on the dance floor. His face looks like a rotten piece of fruit. He's holding a glass of ice in one hand, lurching about, drunk.

BACK TO ROB

who leans in for a closer look. He's incredibly intrigued.

ON THE MONITOR

Behind Moses, Nico's dancing with Jamie in the background!

EXT. TWIN CINEMA - DAY

The banner on the side of the theatre reads: "THROWBACK THURSDAY." Two movie posters hang next to the banner: one is "THE GOOD, THE BAD, AND THE UGLY" and the other, "BLOOD AND BLACK LACE."

Rob walks up to the TICKET SELLER in the box office.

> ROB
> Two for 'Blood and Black Lace.'

EXT. QUICKIE MART - DAY

Rob stands next to a payphone, staring at Jazz's phone number (781-9732) written on a napkin covered in mustard stains.

INTERCUT - TELEPHONE CONVERSATION

> JAZZ
> Hello?

> ROB
> Jazz. Hey, it's me...uh Jimmy.

>   JAZZ
>   (excitedly)
>   Hey, Jimmy! How are you?

>   ROB
>   Ah -- I'm good. I was wondering if
>   you'd like to get together tonight.

EXT. MAIN PIER, TOPSIDE BOARDWALK - NIGHT

Jazz leans over the railing and lights up a new cigarette. Not too far away, Jazz's boss, ERIC, is closing the stand.

Rob sneaks up behind Jazz and gives her a bird-like tap on the shoulder. She turns to an empty space next to her. Then turns to her other side and finds Rob grinning like a goon.

>   JAZZ
>   Hey, Jimmy...

Jazz gives Rob a hug. Then she offers Rob a smoke.

>   ROB
>   I didn't know you smoked.

>   JAZZ
>   (shrugging)
>   Social smoker, I guess.

>   ROB
>   Yeah. Me too.

>   JAZZ
>   I went through a phase where I
>   smoked like a pack or two a day. I
>   know it's terrible for you, like a
>   double-edged sword. But I don't
>   smoke nearly as much any more.
>   Why? Does that turn you off?

>   ROB
>   Nah. I'm not one to judge.

A comfortable silence builds. Rob and Jazz share a smile.

EXT. THE TWIN MOVIE THEATRE - NIGHT

As Rob and Jazz move their way through the crowd, RAUL SUAREZ, 32, pats Rob on the shoulder.

> RAUL
> Jimmy? Is that you?

Rob tilts his head in confusion.

> RAUL (CONT'D)
> It's me, Raul. West Harleton.
> Remember?

Raul opens his arm, as if he's welcoming a hug.

> ROB
> You got the wrong guy.

Raul touches Rob on the arm.

Then, Rob pushes Raul's hand away. Raul throws his hand up in surrender, then backs away.

> JAZZ
> (whispering)
> Who was that guy?

> ROB
> No clue.

INT. HALLWAY, THE TWIN MOVIE THEATRE - NIGHT

Rob and Jazz walk down a dark stretch of hallway lined with movie posters, both old and new. Jazz motions to one poster in particular: "THE TERMINATOR."

> JAZZ
> Not too long ago, I did a movie
> poster for 'Mad Max.'

> ROB
> Oh yeah. Which one?

> JAZZ
> Beyond Thunderdome. It was on
> display for about two weeks or so.

> ROB
> So, you're an artist?

>   JAZZ
> On the side. Yeah. I'd love to do
> it full time, but the competition is
> rather fierce.

>   ROB
> They call it 'starving artist' for a
> reason --

>   JAZZ
> -- Not me...
>   (takes a bite of
>   popcorn)
> ...A girl's gotta eat.

Rob laughs. So does Jazz, even with her mouth full.

INT. THEATRE 2, THE TWIN MOVIE THEATRE - NIGHT

Halfway through "BLOOD AND BLACK LACE," Rob's head starts to bob as if his neck's made out of a spring. Eyelids heavy.

>   ROB
> I'll be back.

>   JAZZ
> Okay.

INT. MEN'S RESTROOM, THE TWIN MOVIE THEATRE - NIGHT

Rob turns on the faucet and splashes his face with water.

>   MOSES (O.S.)
> What the hell are you doing?

Rob moves his eyes up to the mirror where Moses is using the urinal behind him.

>   MOSES (CONT'D)
> Don't you have more pressing issues
> than going to a movie with 'some'
> girl?

>   ROB
> I need the break. You know this --

Moses finishes, shakes it, and glances over his shoulder.

> MOSES
> -- Break? Seriously? Your whole life
> has been one gigantic break.

Rob looks down at his pants to see that water has splashed over his groin. Pissed off, he dries his pants with a towel.

> MOSES (CONT'D)
> Are you ready to get back to work
> or are you going to continue to
> delay the inevitable?

The door SQUEAKS open!

Rob turns to the MOVIEGOER entering the restroom. Turns back to Moses. He's gone. Only a wadded tissue on the floor...

INT. RUBY'S APARTMENT - NIGHT

Ruby places the set of keys on his desk where the contents of Rob's chest are all laid out.

Contents include surveillance PHOTOS of Conrad taken from a distance, logs, reports, statements, interviews, thorough profiles on each suspect involved in the shooting, and then, finally, an arsenal of weapons, mainly handguns and knives.

Ruby grabs a beer from the fridge and slides a VHS tape into the VCR player on top of the TV.

ON THE SCREEN

Grainy surveillance footage of Moses sneaking out of Red Pines. Creeping around orderlies. Moses moves quickly from one hallway to the next, almost cat-like, rehearsed.

BACK TO RUBY

who leans in closer to the TV and watches in astonishment.

INT. THEATRE 2, THE TWIN MOVIE THEATRE - NIGHT

Rob walks back to his seat where Jazz is engulfed in the movie. Hesitates at first. Then he leans close to her.

> ROB
> Let's get outta here.

>   JAZZ
> For real?

>   ROB
> Yeah.

>   JAZZ
> Are you okay?

Rob nods. Then Jazz rolls up the half-eaten bag of popcorn, stuffs it in her oversized purse, and takes it with her.

EXT. TOPSIDE BEACH - NIGHT

Rob and Jazz walk side by side on the dark beach, the strong ocean gust cutting through their hair.

>   JAZZ
> Do you have any dreams?

>   ROB
> Of course I have dreams.

>   JAZZ
> Like what?

>   ROB
> What do I dream of?

Jazz smiles, leans close to Rob in a partial hug.

>   JAZZ
> No, silly. I mean, like, do you have
> any dreams in life? Any aspirations?
> You know?

>   ROB
> I don't know. I guess I'd like to
> maybe one day have a family.

>   JAZZ
> Oh -- okay. What else?

>   ROB
> What else?

> JAZZ
> Yeah. I think everybody eventually
> has a family at some point in his or
> her life. Right?

Rob holds his head downward, doesn't answer.

> JAZZ (CONT'D)
> What do you want to do with your
> life?

> ROB
> I thought about becoming a nurse.
> I might get back into that.

> JAZZ
> What stopped you?

Rob pauses, thinks.

> ROB
> Lost interest, I guess.

> JAZZ
> It's good money from what I hear.
> And good hours, too. You only
> work like four days a week --

> ROB
> -- How about you? What do you
> wanna do?

> JAZZ
> Me? Hotelier.

Rob turns to a baffled Jazz.

> ROB
> (holding in a laugh)
> Hotelier? Really?

> JAZZ
> I'm gonna build my own hotel off
> the coast of San Nicolás. Then, I'm
> gonna call it 'The Galleria.' It'll be
> one of the finest hotels in southern
> California. I'll even hang my
> artwork in the lobby for all my
> wonderful guests to see.

                ROB
Well, whenever you open 'The
Galleria,' I'll make sure I'm your first
guest.

Jazz turns her gaze to the mansions along the shore in NEW TOWN. She grabs
Rob by the hand. Jerks her head in a nod.

                JAZZ
I have an idea.

She takes off toward a luxurious mansion.

                ROB
           (following Jazz)
Where are you going?

                JAZZ
It's a surprise!

EXT. RUSSO'S MANSION/POOL - NIGHT

Rob tries to keep up with Jazz as she treks up a steep pathway. They come across
a fancy pool behind the unlit mansion. Jazz doesn't waste any time removing her
clothes.

                ROB
Jazz? Seriously? What are you
doing? We're gonna get in trouble.

                JAZZ
           (shrugging)
It's better than coffee. <u>And</u> it beats
going to the public pool...

Jazz strips down to her undies, places her clothes, as well as her phone aside, and
leaps into the pool. Rob follows suit. Undresses. Carefully places his clothes
behind an azalea. Dives feet-first into ritzy pool.

                ROB
Wow! That's cold!

                JAZZ
It's perfect.

Rob and Jazz both tread water, quietly and calmly. Rob swims closer to Jazz,
shivering from the coldness of the water.

As Rob advances closer to Jazz for a kiss, the LIGHTS inside the mansion
suddenly turn on!

Jazz quickly grabs Rob by the arm and ducks into the water. They swim to the side of the wall closest to the mansion.

While underneath the water, Rob can't keep his eyes off Jazz. Her eyes like a cat, cutting through him. She tilts her head, like a cat does whenever it's confused or intrigued.

Jazz's eyes roll upward to the shadowy figure looming over the water; pulls Rob close to her until the shadow fades away. Then, the lights turn off; and they both surface.

Rob inches his head above the pool. A brawny man wearing a JUMPSUIT strolls back inside the mansion. Closes door.

> ROB
> (relievedly)
> Close call.

EXT. NEW TOWN BEACH - NIGHT

As Jazz washes the chlorine from her hair underneath the shower, Rob picks up her purse. He grabs a crinkled photo of Jazz sticking out of the side pocket: Jazz, a couple of years younger, overweight, borderline obese. He looks at Jazz, looks at the photo, then, once more, looks at Jazz.

She cuts off the shower, her eyes sealed shut from the dripping water. She wrings the water from her hair.

As Jazz opens her eyes, Rob's standing before her, handing both her clothes and purse to her.

> JAZZ
> (cutely)
> Thanks.

INT. ROB'S HONDA CIVIC - NIGHT

Rob carefully slides his hand over Jazz's knee.

> JAZZ
> (breaking the
> silence)
> Listen, Jimmy --

                              ROB
                    (removing his hand)
              -- I had a great time tonight.

Jazz giggles from the awkwardness of the conversation.

                              JAZZ
              Yeah. So did I.

                              ROB
              You have any plans tomorrow?

                              JAZZ
              Well, I work in the afternoon.
              Other than that, I don't...
                    (abruptly)
              ...Hey! You should swing by the
              stand, if you're not too busy.

                              ROB
              Yeah. I might do that.

                              JAZZ
              I'll even hook you up with a
              cinnamon pretzel.

                              ROB
              Don't tell Eric.

                              JAZZ
              If Eric only knew half the things I
              did behind his back...

Rob clears his throat, both hands shaking. Jazz leans over the center console and kisses Rob on the cheek.

                              JAZZ (CONT'D)
              I'll talk to you soon.

Rob nods.

                              JAZZ (CONT'D)
              Good night.

                              ROB
              Yeah. Good night.

INT. BALCONY, THE FORESHORE HOTEL - NIGHT

While smoking a cigarette, Rob stands against the railing and stares at the Pacific Ocean covered in pale moonlight.

INT. SURVEILLANCE ROOM, CRYSTAL PALACE - NIGHT

In front of a row of monitors stands BISHOP, early 50's, poorly done face lift, which makes his face look more freakish than natural.

>   BISHOP (O.S.)
>   Argento. Call Nico for me.

ON THE SCREEN

With a drink in his hand, Moses sits at the end of the bar.

BACK IN THE SURVEILLANCE ROOM

Behind Bishop stands his steely-faced assistant, ARGENTO, 29, as reverent as a Queen's Guard.

>   BISHOP (CONT'D)
>   Tell him he has a visitor.

INT. HOTEL ROOM, THE FORESHORE HOTEL - DAY

Rob violently wakes up to the BLAST of a gunshot!

Sweating profusely, he checks the door to see a petite MAID standing behind the peephole, her eyes bug-eyed, like a fish, her head blown out of proportion.

>   ROB
>   (weakly)
>   Ah -- Please come back later.

He checks the time on the TV: 10:44 AM. Peeks through the peephole where the maid strolls her cart to the next room.

INT. BATHROOM, HOTEL ROOM - DAY

Rob finishes vomiting, removes his face from the toilet, and flushes the toilet. Then splashes his face with water.

INT. BILL'S GADGETS AND ELECTRONICS - NIGHT

Rob pays the shady CASHIER for a pre-paid cell phone -- better known as a BURNER -- with only cash.

EXT. PARKING LOT, THE STRIP - NIGHT

After pacing around his car, Rob decides to call Jazz.

INT. JAZZ'S BEDROOM, APARTMENT - CONTINUOUS

Jazz's phone glows. She peels the headphones from her ears. Stops working on the "FREAK" poster. Answers the call.

> JAZZ
> Hello?

INTERCUT - PHONE CONVERSATION

> ROB
> Hey, it's me, Jimmy.

> JAZZ
> Hey, Jimmy! What are you up to?

> ROB
> Oh, nothing much. I was meaning
> to visit you at work, but I've been
> under the weather all day.

> JAZZ
> Is everything okay?

> ROB
> Yeah. Now I am. Must've been
> something I ate, I guess.

> JAZZ
> I'm glad you're feeling better.

> ROB
> Thanks. So, what are you doing
> right now?

INT. BATHROOM, HOTEL ROOM - NIGHT

Smiling from ear to ear, Rob scrubs the shampoo from his hair and makes sure not to miss a spot. Everything is perfect.

INT. THE LIQUOR STORE - NIGHT

As Rob counts the money for the Cuervo, he pauses in thought.

> CLERK (O.S.)
> Twelve-fifty.

Rob ignores the clerk.

                         CLERK (CONT'D)
          Sir?

                         ROB
          Ah. Forget about it.

Rob leaves the bottle on the counter and rushes out of the store. Neither upset nor discouraged; however, he's surprisingly at ease with himself.

EXT. PARKING LOT - CONTINUOUS

As Rob strolls toward his car, two shadows, as slender as street poles, emerge from behind.

In the reflection of his car's window, two figures rise over his shoulder. He hears a CLICK, then...

The barrel of a handgun is pressed against the backside of Rob's head before he can spin around.

                         THUG'S VOICE (O.S.)
          Give me your fuckin' money, bitch!

As Rob tries to turn his shoulder, a black gloved hand forces his head the other way.

                         THUG'S VOICE (O.S.) (CONT'D)
          Did I say you can turn around,
          muthafucka? Give me the money
          now!

The thug HITS Rob in the backside of his head with the butt of the handgun.

Rob stumbles forward and HITS the side of the car. Manages to sneak a peek at the two FACES partially hidden underneath white bandanas with black paisley print...

INT. CRYSTAL PALACE - NIGHT - FLASHBACK

Drew splits with Rob and Flip as they shoulder their way through a crowd. Drew's BLUE EYES slowly cross Rob's range of vision like the eyes of an insect. A primitive thing.

EXT. PARKING LOT - NIGHT - PRESENT DAY

The same BLUE EYES behind the white bandana. Rob draws his eyes toward the blue cast on Drew's arm...

INT. PATIO, NICO'S BEACH HOUSE - NIGHT - FLASHBACK

Drew spills Rob's beer all over Jamie. Then Drew throws a drunken punch at Rob but Rob quickly counters by ducking and grabbing Drew's arm and then...

CRACK!

Drew hollers out in great agony as he cradles his broken arm, as if it's a newborn baby.

EXT. PARKING LOT - NIGHT - PRESENT DAY

As Rob attempts to stand, Drew strikes Rob across the face with the blue cast, dazing him. Then he unzips his fly and urinates on Rob's bloody face.

> THUG
> Say cheese, bitch!

The thug takes a photo with the camera on his phone. Then Drew steals the Rolex. Pockets the money from Rob's wallet.

INT. BATHROOM, THE FORESHORE HOTEL - NIGHT

Rob SLAMS the door behind him and storms to the sink. He checks his injuries. Hands trembling with rage. He steadies his hands, washes the blood and urine from his face.

INT. HOTEL ROOM, THE FORESHORE HOTEL - CONTINUOUS

Once Rob's all clean, he pulls the burner from his pocket and stares at Jazz's number, tempting to hit the TALK button. His limbs loosen. He falls to his knees, cups his face, and cries into the palms of his hands.

INT. BALCONY, THE FORESHORE HOTEL - NIGHT

Rob listens to the sea before him. Takes in slow, deep breaths and tries his best to keep calm.

EXT. PARKING LOT - NIGHT - FLASHBACK

Drew towers over an injured Rob. Part of the bandana creases upward from the smile rising on Drew's face.

INT. INTERNET CAFE, CYBER JAXX'S - NIGHT - PRESENT DAY

Rob opens Flip's Instagram page.

ON THE MONITOR

A photo of Rob lying on the asphalt, all bloody, both of his hands shielding his face. Over four thousand LIKES. Flip replies to one of the many comments:

> "That's my boy, DRU DOG, from
> the Crazy, CRAZY Cru taking a piss
> on sum lil' punk ass bitch."

BACK TO ROB

who clinches his teeth in rage.

INT. RUBY'S APARTMENT - NIGHT

Ruby searches through the contents inside Rob's chest. One item in particular piques his interest. It's an evidence log. The signature at the bottom: DWIGHT ARLINGTON.

EXT. DWIGHT'S LAKE HOUSE - DAY

Ruby parks in front of the house surrounded by dense woods.

INT. KITCHEN, DWIGHT'S LAKE HOUSE - DAY

Rob's friend, DWIGHT ARLINGTON, 50's, dapper, handsome, a meat and potatoes kind of man, guides Ruby to the table.

                         DWIGHT
               Can I offer you any coffee,
               Detective?

                         RUBY
               No thanks...
                    (sitting down)
                         (MORE)

> RUBY (CONT'D)
> ...You know Robert Backer through his father. Correct?

> DWIGHT
> That's right. Before Tom retired, we worked at the same precinct. He was one of the good ones.

Dwight places the evidence sheet on the table.

> RUBY
> Did Thomas know that Ayker was accepting bribes from Conrad West in order to keep quiet about the prostitution ring inside Daddy's Playground?

Dwight turns away, thinks, then squares himself to Ruby.

> DWIGHT
> Do you have a family, John? Any children?

> RUBY
> No.

Dwight walks to the window and stares at the lake outside.

> DWIGHT
> When Robert came to me asking for help, I knew that if I helped him I could no longer wear the badge.

> RUBY
> Why didn't Robert turn to his father for help?

> DWIGHT
> He wasn't exactly 'close' to Tom.

> RUBY
> And Robert was closer to you?

> DWIGHT
> Tom was like a brother to me, and it was our duty to look after one another no matter what the cost;
> (MORE)

                              DWIGHT (CONT'D)
however, we knew that there would
come a day when we would be on
our own. When that day came, we
wouldn't be able to protect one
another...
         (facing Ruby)
...You really want to go down this
road, Detective?

                              RUBY
What other choice do I have?

EXT. THE AMAZING PRETZEL STAND, TOPSIDE BOARDWALK - DAY

Rob, who's wearing the Rolex with a small crack in the glass casing, stops by the
stand where Eric's wiping down the counter with a damp rag.

                              ERIC
How can I help you, sir?

                              ROB
I was actually looking for Jazz.

Eric stops what he's doing. His face slackens in a vacant expression. Squares his
shoulders to Rob.

                              ERIC
         (bitterly)
Ah-ha. So, you must be Jimmy.

                              ROB
Yeah.

                              ERIC
She called in sick.

Eric proceeds to wipe down the counter.

INT. ROB'S HONDA CIVIC - DAY

Frustrated, Rob steps inside the car. Slams the door.

CLICK!

In the rear view mirror a revolver is being aimed at his ear.

                              MOSES (O.S.)
You don't listen. Do you?

In the backseat sits Moses, his left arm draped in a sling.

>   ROB
> What the hell happened to you?

>   MOSES
> Fell.

Moses flicks the barrel toward the front of the car.

>   MOSES (CONT'D)
> Drive.

Rob puts the gear in DRIVE.

>   ROB
> Where are we going?

>   MOSES
> You mean, where are <u>you</u> going?

No response from Rob as he starts to drive away.

>   MOSES (CONT'D)
> You have somewhere you should be
> right now. Instead, you're off trick
> or treating with a girl you barely
> even know...
>   (pointing to the
>   right)
> ...Take a right here.

>   ROB
> Why are you following me?

Rob and Moses share an icy glare in the rear view mirror; then Moses turns to the window, gazes outside.

>   MOSES
> How many times have I covered
> your ass?

>   ROB
> You know, I was doing just fine
> before you showed up.

>   MOSES
> Really? Tied down to a bed at
> night? Forced to take medication.
> That's you doing 'just fine'? Turn
> left at the stoplight.

Rob stops behind a car at the stoplight.

> MOSES (CONT'D)
> If I didn't break you out of that
> hellhole, you'd still be there rotting
> away. <u>That's</u> the truth.

Rob glances at his knuckles, bruised and swollen.

> MOSES (O.S.) (CONT'D)
> Sooner or later, you're going to have
> to learn how to accept the truth for
> what it is.

EXT. FIFTH CIRCLE STREET - CONTINUOUS

Rob turns left at the stoplight.

INT. ROB'S HONDA CIVIC - CONTINUOUS

Rob turns his eyes toward the rear view mirror.

> ROB
> (scornfully)
> Let me ask you something. Why
> do you care so much about my
> business?

> MOSES
> The sooner you find the people
> responsible for Jimmy's death, the
> sooner you can do me <u>my</u> favor.

> ROB
> What's the favor?

Moses points left. Puts down the revolver. Sighs.

> MOSES
> Left. Right here.

Moses hands Rob a baseball cap, a pair of cheap Aviator sunglasses, and a small
bottle of makeup.

> MOSES (CONT'D)
> Clearly, <u>he</u> can't see you the way you
> are. Otherwise, your cover will be
> blown.

Rob turns to the softball field where Nico's playing.

EXT. MCDOWELL PARK - DAY

Rob takes a seat on the bleachers and watches Nico play cheerleader with the team. Along the field are droves of gorgeous women dressed in provocative baseball clothing.

Nico waves down Rob across the field, breaks free from the team, runs to Rob. Both Of them slap hands.

                    NICO
          Glad you came out, brother.

                    ROB
          Had nothing else better to do.

Nico points at Rob's attire.

                    NICO
          You look like you're related to the
          Unabomber.

Rob grabs the bill of his hat. Laughs.

                    ROB
          Oh, this? Me and the sun don't get
          along too well.

                    NICO
          I used to be the same way when I
          had really bad acne. Dermatologist
          put me on this medicine that made
          my skin sensitive. Couldn't go out
          in the sun without lotion or a hat.

                    ROB
          Fair skin, I guess.

                    NICO
          A'ight, man. Whatever.

Nico backpedals his way into the outfield. Grins.

                    NICO (CONT'D)
                (holding out his
                hands)
          If you wanna ball, just grab a glove.
          You're welcome to join or you can
          just watch. Up to you.

                    ROB
          I'll just watch.

NICO

You're choice, brother...

INT. INTERNET CAFE, CYBER JAXX'S - DAY

Rob types in the words NEW TOWN DRAGONS in the search engine. Clicks on a link, which takes him to LINKEDIN pages.

ON THE MONITOR

The words SOFTWARE DEVELOPER and PROGRAMMER. One company stands out, the most recent company: VERSION DEVELOPERS.

BACK TO ROB

who searches the words VERSION DEVELOPERS. Clicks on the company's website. Scrolls down a list of clients until he comes across the brand "THE PLEASURESABER^{TM}."

ROB

PleasureSaber. That's it.

INT. NICO'S BEACH HOUSE - NIGHT

Rob makes his way through a wild crowd of partygoers dancing in the LIVING ROOM. Rubbing shoulders with the wealthiest of New Town. He breaks away from the crowd. He heads toward the PATIO where it's less crazy and noisy.

EXT. PATIO, NICO'S BEACH HOUSE - CONTINUOUS

Rob lights up a cigarette and passes a mixture of giggly men and women hanging out underneath a CANOPY, then a massive fire pit where other rowdier partygoers are chilling and smoking from all kinds of different drugs and whatnot.

Then Rob comes across an infinity pool where a couple of anorexic girls are skinny-dipping, Jazz being one of the girls swimming in the pool!

Rob does a double take at Jazz, who happens to be a girl who looks similar to Jazz but she's <u>not</u> his Jazz.

As Rob makes his way to the bar, he BUMPS into Nico, causing him to slip and fall on his left shoulder!

NICO

Fuck! Jimmy! I'm so sorry...

With his clothes soaking wet, Nico tends to Rob.

> NICO (CONT'D)
> ...You okay, buddy?

> ROB
> Fine.

> NICO
> (helping Rob stand)
> Sorry, man. You came out of
> fucking nowhere.

Nico points at a stark naked SASHA with a ball python coiled around her wrist, skin as creamy white as a porcelain doll and hair as dark as the feathers of a raven.

> NICO (CONT'D)
> Sasha was chasing me with that
> goddamn snake -- I hate fuckin'
> snakes. I turned around for a split
> second and then, when I turned
> back around --

> ROB
> -- It's all good. It happens.

Nico pats Rob on the arm, dusts off his shoulders.

> NICO
> (laughing)
> It's not your week. Is it?

> ROB
> I've had better days.

Nico inches closer to Rob, then nods at the slim Latino, YOLANDA, sitting on the edge of the pool.

> NICO
> FYI: Yolanda was talking about you.

> ROB
> Oh yeah?

> NICO
> She thinks you're -- and I'm quoting
> her -- a 'real' cutie.
> (MORE)

                        NICO (CONT'D)
            Why don't you give me a hand
            downstairs and I'll introduce you to
            her in a minute. What do you say?

INT. PARKING GARAGE, NICO'S BEACH HOUSE - NIGHT

Nico flips on the light switch. Points to a nook.

                        NICO
            The kegs are right over here.

As Nico moves toward the kegs, he stops in his tracks.

                        NICO (CONT'D)
                    (snapping his
                        fingers)
            I almost forgot!

He pulls out Rob's switchblade from his back pocket.

                        NICO (CONT'D)
            I believe this belongs to you.

He hands the switchblade to Rob.

                        ROB
            Must've dropped it. Thanks, man.

                        NICO
            I haven't seen one of those in
            fuckin' ages.

                        ROB
            Never know when you might need
            it.

                        NICO
            Well, from the way you handled
            that one 'jerk' the other night,
            you're probably better off without
            it.

Rob studies Nico as he maneuvers his way around the kegs.

                        NICO (CONT'D)
            Don't you worry. That'll be the last
            time he's invited over here. And
            you won't need...
                    (pointing at blade)
            ...that here. Believe me.

Rob pockets the switchblade.

> ROB
> (grabbing his
> stomach)
> Say, where's the bathroom?

INT. HALLWAY, NICO'S BEACH HOUSE - NIGHT

With his game face on, Rob passes a dark room at the end of the hallway. He flips a switch. Creeps inside.

INT. STORAGE ROOM, NICO'S BEACH HOUSE - CONTINUOUS

Cardboard boxes line the walls. Rob inspects the cardboard boxes with the words PLEASURESABER written on the side. Opens one of the boxes with his switchblade. He pulls out a DILDO the size of a donkey's dick from a black tube.

As Rob places the sex toy back in the box and leaves the room, he BUMPS into Nico again!

> NICO
> You find what you were looking
> for?

> ROB
> The bathroom. Yeah.

Nico peeks at the open box over Rob's shoulder.

> NICO
> I also see you found my gold at the
> end of the rainbow.

Rob's hand eases toward the switchblade behind his back.

> ROB
> Oh! That...
> (facing Nico)
> ...It's really none of my business
> what you do in your spare time.

> NICO
> Don't be so naive, Jimmy. Sex _is_
> my business.

Nico walks Rob back into the ROOM. Pulls out a sex toy.

NICO (CONT'D)
I tell you, people can't get enough of
these things. I swear they sell like
hotcakes.

ROB
You sell this stuff?

NICO
Of course. What'd you think I did
for a living? Manage a nightclub?

ROB
Like I said, none of my business.

NICO
Starting out was the hardest part,
then, once the product started to
catch on and the word got out...
        (grinning)
...that's all she wrote.

ROB
I didn't know dildos were in such
high demand these days --

NICO
-- Not just any dildo, Jimmy.

Nico untwists the other end of the toy. Similar to a male masturbatory toy with
one side being the sleeve of an artificial vagina.

NICO (CONT'D)
For her on one side. For him on
the other.

ROB
So, what got you into the 'pleasure'
business?

NICO
Honestly, if I had one of these when
I was a kid, I'd probably never leave
my bedroom. And -- between you
and me -- I probably would've never
picked up crabs from my high
school crush Charlotte Web.

ROB
Charlotte Web? Like the --

> NICO
> -- like the book. True story, man.
> Her parents must've had a sense of
> humor when they named their
> daughter after the children's book,
> 'CHARLOTTE'S WEB'. I
> remember after Charlotte, I didn't
> touch a girl in like four months.
> Almost scarred me for life.

Nico laughs. So does Rob.

> NICO (CONT'D)
> (handing Rob the
> device)
> If you close your eyes, it almost feels
> like the real thing. Plus, it glows in
> the dark.

> ROB
> Get outta here.

EXT. PATIO, NICO'S BEACH HOUSE - NIGHT

Rob and Nico are sharing a laugh while they carry the keg toward another clique
of partygoers. One man in particular stands out: Bishop, wearing an expensive
suit, dark hair slicked back, gray streaks on the side.

Nico nods at Bishop, who, in return, nods back. Nico and Rob set down the keg
near the fire pit. They approach Bishop.

> NICO
> This is the guy I was talking about
> the other day --

> BISHOP
> -- James. Am I right?

Rob coyly nods his head <u>yes</u>.

> ROB
> You can call me Jimmy.

> BISHOP
> Nico has told me a lot about you.

Bishop holds out his hand, but Rob doesn't shake it.

> BISHOP (CONT'D)
> Surely, you must have a full name,
> Jimmy --

                              ROB
          -- Jimmy. Just Jimmy.

                            BISHOP
          Okay, Just Jimmy.
                    (motioning to Nico)
          Kind of like the musician. That
          one smooth cat -- What's his name?

                          NICO (O.S.)
          -- You mean Prince.

                            BISHOP
          That's the one. No last name. Just
          one name. I like that.

Bishop smirks at Rob, then glances down at his lonely hand. Finally, Rob shakes
his hand.

                        BISHOP (CONT'D)
          Luther Bishop, owner of Crystal
          Palace.

A QUICK FLASH of Bishop, clothes waterlogged from the rain, as he stands next
to James on the bridge in Old Town.

Rob removes his hand from Bishop's hand.

                              ROB
          Pleasure to meet you.

EXT. TOPSIDE BEACH - DAY

Rob moves farther out into the sea, skipping over each wave as they roll by him.
He draws his attention toward the sky above. The clouds have given way to a pale
blue sky.

INT. LIVING ROOM, NICO'S BEACH HOUSE - DAY

The doorbell rings!

Nico wakes, super-hungover. He pushes aside a couple of naked bodies, both
men and women. Stumbles to the front door. Opens the door. Before Nico
stands Ruby.

EXT. MAIN STREET, TOPSIDE - DAY

As Rob walks along the sidewalk, his burner RINGS in his pocket. He flips open
the burner, the caller ID reads "NICO." Rob answers the call.

                              ROB
          Hello.

                              NICO (V.O.)
          What's up, Doc?

                              ROB
          Sup, Nico.

                              NICO (V.O.)
          Chilling, man. Some night last
          night, huh?

                              ROB
          Tell me about it. I can't remember
          a damn thing --

                              NICO (V.O.)
          -- What are you doing right now?

Rob looks up at the sign, "CYBER JAXX'S."

                              ROB
          Just killing time.

                              NICO (V.O.)
          I'm free for about an hour, if you
          wanna get up.

                              ROB
          Sure. Okay.

INT. MEN'S RESTROOM, THE PALM TREE HOTEL - DAY

Rob splashes his face with water, then pulls out the switchblade from his back
pocket. Looks it over. Then, he tosses the switchblade in the trash can on his
way out.

EXT. THE PALM TREE HOTEL - DAY

In his blue Lambo, Nico drives up the entrance ramp where Rob's standing in the
lobby. Rob, as calm as a saint, walks from the revolving doors. Waves hello to
Nico.

                              NICO
          Sup, playa?

                              ROB
          Sup.

Rob hops inside the Lambo and marvels at the interior.

> ROB (CONT'D)
> Holy shit. This is freakin' nice.

> NICO
> Wait till I get her on the road.

EXT. PACIFIC COAST HIGHWAY - DAY

The blue Lambo ZOOMS past cars, as if each one's an obstacle!

INT. NICO'S LAMBO - CONTINUOUS

Rob checks the speedometer, which reads well above the legal speed limit. He grows worried from Nico's erratic driving.

> NICO
> Wanna hear her purr?

> ROB
> Let's see what she's got, <u>playa</u>.

Rob grips the armrests while Nico easily breaks a hundred!

EXT. TRADER'S INLET - DAY

Nico parks along a cliff overlooking the Pacific Ocean. Nico steps out first while Rob hangs back. Waiting.

INT. NICO'S LAMBO - CONTINUOUS

As Nico starts to walk toward the cliff, Rob checks the glove box where inside a Beretta M9 is tucked underneath a couple of receipts and owner manuals.

> NICO (O.S.)
> You coming, Jimmy?

Rob closes the glove box and steps out of the Lambo.

EXT. TRADER'S INLET - CONTINUOUS

Rob follows Nico to the cliff where they sit on a flat rock.

                    NICO
            (gazing at the sea)
        No matter how hard we try to fuck
        up the Pacific with oil leaks,
        pollution, or whatever garbage we
        dump into it, somehow it'll always
        find a way to bounce back and
        revert to what it's good at doing:
        staying blue, unspoiled...

                    ROB
        Nature has a strange way of
        balancing itself out.

                    NICO
        You got that right.

Nico tosses a pebble into the sea below. Then hangs his head, as if his mind's
heavy with thoughts.

                    NICO (CONT'D)
        Listen, Jimmy, I know what it's like
        to start over with nothing...
            (shuffling pebbles
            below)
        ...I remember when I was in my
        twenties I stayed with my grandma
        in Montana. She and my grandpa
        were separated, and it was just her
        living in the middle of nowhere.

Nico laughs, but he keeps it to himself.

                    NICO (CONT'D)
        I had no phone. No TV. No
        friends. No <u>girl</u>. The first week, I
        almost went crazy.

                    ROB
        I bet.

                    NICO
        After a couple of weeks, I realized
        something about myself.

                    ROB
        What's that?

                    NICO
          I <u>hated</u> myself. Most importantly, I
          hated what I had become.

Nico gets quiet. So does Rob.

                    NICO (CONT'D)
          In a way, I wasn't visiting my
          grandma. I was looking for him...

                    ROB
          Looking for who?

                    NICO
               (seriously)
          My father.

Rob's face goes slack and vacant. He gathers himself.

                    ROB
          Did you ever find him?

                    NICO
          Yeah. I found him all right, but not
          in Montana.

Nico takes a moment to gather himself.

                    NICO (CONT'D)
          When they discovered his body, he
          was lying against a redwood with a
          bullet hole in his head. We couldn't
          even have an open casket at his
          funeral.

                    ROB
          Sorry to hear --

                    NICO
          -- Don't be. The man was a <u>liar</u>, a
          <u>thief</u>, a <u>criminal</u>...
               (holding out three
                    fingers)
          ...You know only three people
          showed up for his funeral. Three!

>   ROB
> I guess you find out who really
> misses you once you're dead.
>
>   NICO
> You know if I didn't spend that
> time in Montana before I found out
> about his death, I never would've
> found what I <u>truly</u> wanted.
>
>   ROB
> What did you want?
>
>   NICO
>   (clearly)
> Closure.

Nico turns away from Rob and stares at the Pacific Ocean.

EXT. THE PALM TREE HOTEL - DAY

Nico pulls up to the entrance ramp. Rob slaps hands with Nico. Steps out.
Closes door. Walks away.

>   NICO (O.S.)
> Yo, Jimmy!

Rob pauses, turns around, walks back to the Lambo, and leans through the open
passenger window.

>   NICO (CONT'D)
> So, I'll see you around.
>
>   ROB
> Yeah. I'm not going anywhere.
>
>   NICO
> Take care of yourself, Jimmy.

Rob nods goodbye. Then Nico speeds away.

INT. COMPUTER AREA, PUBLIC LIBRARY - DAY

Rob clicks on an article from the BRIAR CANYON GAZETTE.

ON THE MONITOR

The headline: "BODY IDENTIFIED AS LOCAL RECLUSE CONRAD
WEST."

At the bottom of the page: a photo of a content Conrad with his arm wrapped around his annoyed son, Nico, early teens.

EXT. BRIDGE, OLD TOWN - DAY

Rob arrives at the scene of the crime, then walks down an embankment, then cautiously makes his way down a steep hill.

EXT. RIVER - DAY - FLASHBACK SEQUENCE

Rob, who <u>appears</u> the same age, rushes through a crowd of bystanders, dodges police officers, trying to make his way to a motionless James being hoisted onto a stretcher by the paramedics. His brother's clinging to life. Nearly dead.

EXT. SHORE, RIVER - DAY - PRESENT DAY

Rob stands at the same spot where James's body was found.

EXT. SHORE, RIVER - DAY - FLASHBACK SEQUENCE

Rob kneels down and grabs the necklace with the golden pendant of a wing chained around a tarnished industrial pipe, which had taken root. He holds the necklace in his palm.

INT. MOTEL ROOM, COMFORT STAY - NIGHT - PRESENT DAY

Rob stares at the burner in his hand. Contemplates.

Copies of BRIAR CANYON local newspaper articles about Conrad West's "SUICIDE," as well as his death record, are spread out on the bed behind Rob.

> REPORTER (ON TV)
> Coroners found lethal amounts of
> opiates in Foster's bloodstream...

Rob grabs the remote and turns up the volume on the TV.

ON THE SCREEN

A blown up photo of Anthony Foster's ugly mug.

REPORTER (ON TV) (CONT'D)
...So far, police have ruled Foster's
death as an accident.

INT. ROB'S HONDA CIVIC - NIGHT

Rob cruises by Crystal Palace. He stops at the stoplight across the nightclub.
Stares at the cruiser parked in the parking lot. The light turns GREEN. Then,
Rob drives away.

EXT. THE AMAZING PRETZEL STAND, TOPSIDE BOARDWALK -
NIGHT

Rob stops by the pretzel stand where Eric's closing up. Eric shakes his head no
before Rob can utter a single word.

INT. ROB'S HONDA CIVIC - NIGHT

Rob waits outside Jazz's apartment. Checks his face, as well as his hair, in the
mirror. Sighs. Then exits the car.

EXT. JAZZ'S APARTMENT - NIGHT

Jazz answers the door in tight black leggings and a black "DRAGONBALL Z" tee
cut an inch above her innie belly button.

                    JAZZ
          (sharply)
     Jimmy? What are you doing here?

                    ROB
     I...I was just in the neighborhood.

Jazz shifts her weight to one side of her body.

                    ROB (CONT'D)
     I talked to Eric, your boss. He said
     you don't work there anymore.

                    JAZZ
     It was only short term. Besides, I
     went back to another job that pays
     better than minimum wage.

Jazz crosses her arms over her chest.

                    ROB
     That's cool. So, where --

> JAZZ
> -- What happened the other night?

Rob turns to his left, struggling to look Jazz in the eye.

> ROB
> (depressingly)
> It's a long story. I should've called
> you. I actually came here to
> apologize --

> JAZZ
> (studying Rob's face)
> -- Did someone hurt you?

The shadow of a person builds on a distant wall behind Jazz. Then Phyllis pokes her head from the KITCHEN.

> PHYLLIS
> Jasper? Who you talking to?

> JAZZ
> (over her shoulder)
> Just a friend.

Jazz blocks the doorway as she squares herself to Rob.

> ROB
> You wanna get outta here?

> JAZZ
> Give me a sec. Will you?

She closes the door while Rob walks back to his car.

EXT. TOPSIDE BOARDWALK - NIGHT

Jazz nibbles from a hot dog while Rob sips from a milkshake.

> ROB
> So, what's this new job? Well, old
> job.

Jazz clears her throat. Swallows carefully.

> JAZZ
> (hesitantly)
> It's like a modeling gig.

> ROB
> Modeling, huh? I can see that. You
> have the look.

                                      JAZZ
               It's okay, I guess. The money's not
               bad. However, there's a lot of
               upkeep, if you know what I mean.

                                          ROB
               So, if like someone dyed your hair
               green and shaved your eyebrows
               while you were sleeping, I supposed
               that wouldn't be good...

                                        JAZZ
               No! Looking like a Chia Pet would
               most certainly <u>not</u> be good!

Rob laughs. Then, eventually, Jazz laughs as well.

INT. PASSENGER CAR, FERRIS WHEEL - NIGHT

Rob slowly interlocks his hand with Jazz's hand.

                                        ROB
               I'm glad you came out.

                                        JAZZ
                  (softly)
               Me too.

EXT. SHERBET'S ICE-CREAM PARLOR - NIGHT

As Rob and Jazz walk in a calm silence, they pass a TV airing a NEWS
conference. Rob stops walking. Then Jazz.

ON THE SCREEN

In front of the courthouse packed with news REPORTERS stands DANIEL
AYKER, 50's, wearing a similar Rolex as Rob's.

                                AYKER (ON TV)
               As your next sheriff, I promise you I
               will make it my number one
               priority to clean up the streets.

BACK TO ROB

who peers closer at the TV.

> JAZZ (O.S.)
> Is something wrong?

A QUICK FLASH of Rob standing by James's bedside. Watching the BREAKING NEWS REPORT. On the TV Cedric is being escorted in handcuffs from his house by cops, one of them being Officer Ayker. Rob turns to the hallway where two icy-looking cops are stationed outside James's hospital room.

Rob snaps from his trance and faces Jazz.

> ROB
> Yeah. I mean, I'm fine. Let's keep
> on walking.

EXT. CIRCUS TENT, TOPSIDE BEACH - NIGHT

On the side of the tent hangs a vintage horror-like poster for the annual "FREAKSPECTACULAR," which begins tomorrow and runs until the end of fall. All of the freaks are on the poster, even Nile, the Snake Man.

> JAZZ
> (showing off the
> poster)
> Check this out...

> ROB
> You did this? No way!

Jazz bashfully shrugs her shoulders.

> ROB (CONT'D)
> You're very talented.

Rob reads the movie credits at the bottom, including Jazz's name, JAZZ CALDWELL, next to the R rated sign.

> ROB (CONT'D)
> Hey! I know her!

Jazz slips her hand around Rob's hand.

> JAZZ
> Come. I wanna show you
> something.

INT. MAIN STAGE, TENT - NIGHT

Jazz guides Rob onto a wooden platform with several contraptions, including the spinning "Wheel of Death;" a table holding a container of knives; then, next to that, a coffin-like box, the "Sawing a woman in half" trick.

She shows Rob a gaudy mirror standing on a secured mount. The frame is lined with brass. Each corner is designed with a lion's paw, and on the top center of the frame is a statue of a lion's head with its eyes shaped with tiny crystals.

> ROB
>> (plainly)
>> It's a mirror.

> JAZZ
> Legend says this special mirror has the power to look <u>inside</u> you, to see what you feel, how you feel, how old you feel, or even how young you feel. And when you look at your reflection, you see exactly what the mirror sees.

> ROB
> Is that right?

> JAZZ
> Go on. Give it a whirl.

Rob stares at the mirror. Doesn't see anything. He turns to Jazz in utter disappointment.

> JAZZ (CONT'D)
> You gotta look harder.

Once more, Rob stares at the mirror. Looks harder. His reflection starts to tremor. He turns away before the reflection can take hold of him...

> JAZZ (CONT'D)
> What did you see?

> ROB
>> (timidly)
>> Na -- nothing.

Rob points out another attraction: a glass jar on top of a wooden post. Inside the jar floats the eyeless head of a corpse, IVORY. She has scales on her face, partially chipped away from age. Her hair looks like old shoelaces dangling from her scalp. Skeletal snakes for hair, the vertebrae of each skeleton fully intact.

> JAZZ
> This is Ivory.

                              ROB
              And what's so special about her?

                              JAZZ
              They say her gaze could turn a man
              into stone.

                              ROB
              Really? They say a lot of things.
              Don't they?

Rob walks closer to a glossy-eyed Jazz wearing very little expression on her face.
He gently grabs her neck and kisses Jazz on the lips. Jazz kisses him back.
Aggressively.

As Rob and Jazz make out, the beam of a FLASHLIGHT shines over the side of
Rob's face.

                        SECURITY GUARD (O.S.)
              Hey! What are you kids doing here?

Rob grabs Jazz's hand, and they take off. The SECURITY GUARD, 40's, out of
shape, chases after them.

EXT. TOPSIDE BOARDWALK - NIGHT

Rob and Jazz lose the security guard in a congested crowd.

EXT. TOPSIDE BEACH - CONTINUOUS

Rob and Jazz catch their breaths. Jazz grabs Rob's hand and places it over her
chest.

                              JAZZ
                        (out of breath)
              My heart is racing.

Rob follows suit, places Jazz's hand over his chest.

                              ROB
              Mine too.

INT. MOTEL ROOM, COMFORT STAY - NIGHT

Rob opens the door for Jazz. He lets her inside the room.

> ROB
>
> Well, this is it.

Jazz takes a quick tour: checks the bathroom, then the sink, then the water stains on the walls.

> JAZZ
>
> It's better than nothin --

Rob makes his move. He starts by making out with Jazz, then removing her shirt. They stumble to the bed and remove their clothes as if they can't get them off quick enough.

INT. SURVELLIANCE ROOM, CRYSTAL PALACE - NIGHT

Nico approaches Bishop from behind. Places a MUG SHOT of Moses on top of one of the monitors, blocking Bishop's view.

> NICO
>
> Did you know anything about this?

Bishop picks up the photo. Callously snorts at the image.

> NICO (CONT'D)
>
> Some cop came to my house, asking
> about him. He's been looking for
> him ever since he escaped from a
> mental institution. A fucking <u>loony
> bin</u>, Luther...

> BISHOP
> (handing the photo
> to Nico)
> What do you want me to tell you,
> Nico?

> NICO
>
> Who is the hell is Robert Backer?

INT. MOTEL ROOM, COMFORT STAY - DAY

A sword of sunlight stretches across the bed and shines over Rob's pale forearm dotted with old needle marks.

Rob wakes and repositions on the bed, but, instead of holding onto Jazz's body, his hand runs across an empty space.

INT. CYBER JAXX'S - DAY

Rob opens Jazz's Facebook page. Checks her latest post.

ON THE MONITOR

A recent selfie of Jazz blowing a kiss for the mirror. She's all dolled up in a black skimpy dress. Very provocative.

EXT. LEMMIE'S DRUG STORE - DAY

Rob pulls out the worn syringe case. He decisively breaks the needle over the curb, then tosses the shattered remains in the trash can. He discards the case as well.

Lastly, Rob dumps the bundle of dope down a sewer drain.

INT. CIRCUS TENT, TOPSIDE BEACH - NIGHT

The emcee, FRAN ROSALIE, 50's, curlicue mustache, welcomes the behemoth, CYRUS, onto the main stage.

> FRAN
> Now, ladies and gentlemen, give a
> warm welcome to the 'Tallest Man
> in the World,' Cyrus!

The hunky EXECUTIONER escorts Cyrus to the "special" mirror, chains the shackles to the stage, then removes the black bag from Cyrus's head.

A pink triangular EYE lights the center of the lion's head. A puff of smoke clouds over Cyrus. The smoke dissipates. Cyrus is no longer standing in front of his reflection; yet, the reflection is a LITTLE PERSON wearing the same clothes, shoes, and hairstyle as Cyrus!

The audience rises in a standing ovation, including Rob and Jazz, both clapping from the magic act. Jazz's phone rings. She checks the number. Touches Rob on the arm.

> JAZZ
> I need to take this.

Jazz shoulders her way through the crowd while Rob watches her walk away. His eyes narrow and darken.

INT. BAR, THE BLUE LOUNGE - NIGHT

Jazz kills her Cranberry and Vodka, then waves down the bartender for another drink. Her phone rings, again, but this time she doesn't answer the call.

Without her acknowledging, Rob watches Jazz closely. Again.

INT. ROB'S HONDA CIVIC - NIGHT

Rob drives past a billboard advertising a brand new sleek and stylish smartcar.

On the billboard: a giant LYNX running alongside the vehicle with a sign that reads, "The New L-Series."

Rob's face melts in deep, serious thought. Then, slack-faced, he turns to a quiet Jazz in the passenger seat.

INT. TOPSIDE BOARDWALK - NIGHT - FLASHBACK (ROB'S MEMORY)

Rob and Jazz stumble from the BAR, Rob preventing Jazz from falling as she sways back and forth from the booze. She accidentally grazes shoulders with a PROSTITUTE.

> JAZZ
> (slurring)
> Make your way for the great Lynda
> Lynx, bitch!

> PROSTITUTE
> Who you calling 'bitch,' bitch?

Rob holds out his hand, trying to keep the peace.

> ROB
> I apologize. She's had one too
> many. Please move on...

> PROSTITUTE (O.S.)
> Well, you better get your woman
> under control!

INT. JAZZ'S BEDROOM - NIGHT - DREAM (KILLING JAZZ)

The tendons in the back of Rob's curled hands look like white cords tied around Jazz's neck. Her eyes swim with panic. She desperately claws at Rob's face, but he shields each strike with his arms. She finally succumbs to Rob's power. Her eyes glaze over and fixate on Rob's red, shaky face.

INT. MOTEL ROOM, THE INN - NIGHT - PRESENT DAY

With one side of his head resting on the pillow, Rob's eyes flick open like the eyes of a creepy doll.

INT. INTERNET CAFE, CYBER JAXX'S - NIGHT

Rob types the words PORN and LYNX in the search engine and scrolls to a
website called "FORCED ENTRY." He takes in a deep breath. Prepares himself.
Then clicks on the link. He scrolls through a gallery of videos on the porn site
until he comes across a "Lynda Lynx" video.

ON THE MONITOR

The caption below one of the videos reads: "Lynda Lynx doin' a forced blowjob."
Other videos: "Lynx takes it in the ass." Another: "Lynx goes hardcore."
Another: "Lynda Lynx ruff doggystyle."

BACK TO ROB

who grabs a pair of headphones and scopes out the cafe, making sure nobody's
watching. He slips on the headphones. Embraces another deep breath. Plays the
first video.

ON THE MONITOR

The cameraman's POV: two crossed legs perched over the top of a cheap
mahogany desk. Then, a KNOCK on the door! The cameraman sets down the
reading material, walks through a well-lit YELLOW ROOM sparse of any
furniture, and peels back a fine beige curtain. He opens the door...

BACK TO ROB

who's leaning closer to the computer.

ON THE MONITOR

Jazz's wearing black-rimmed glasses. School girl's skirt. The camera PANS down
her body and then up her body. A shy Jazz steps inside with her head down and
sits on a couch.

                         CAMERAMAN (O.S.)
            Please state your name for the
            camera.

                              JAZZ
                  (clearing her throat)
            Lynda Lynx.

                         CAMERAMAN (O.S.)
            And how old are you, Ms. Lynx?

>   JAZZ
>   I'm eighteen.

>   CAMERAMAN (O.S.)
>   Is this your first time.

Jazz giggles. Nods her head. Seductive yet innocent.

>   CAMERAMAN (O.S.) (CONT'D)
>   Are you nervous?

>   JAZZ
>   A little.

>   CAMERAMAN (O.S.)
>   Don't be.

The cameraman runs his hand over Jazz's leg.

BACK TO ROB

who's scowling.

Rob fast-forwards the video until Jazz's forced to go down on the cameraman. He struggles to watch as Jazz gags and coughs. Tears falling from his red eyes. Her cheeks smeared with runny mascara. Thick saliva plastered over her chin.

ON THE MONITOR

Jazz's face is being pressed against the floor, the cameraman forcing Jazz to eat her own vomit against her will.

BACK TO ROB

who squeezes the mouse so tightly that it breaks!

Rob removes the headphones and turns his shoulder, only to find Moses sitting right next to him. He appears different, older, frailer, his posture weaker, skin grayer.

>   MOSES
>   Don't you see now?

Rob wipes the tears from his cheek.

>   MOSES (CONT'D)
>   It's time to let her go. Time to
>   finish what you have started...

Moses reaches out and as he places his hand over Rob's shoulder, Rob pushes his arm away.

> ROB
> Get the fuck away from me!

People inside the cafe are now staring at Rob.

> MOSES
> I didn't say it was going to be easy,
> Robert --

Rob rushes to the restroom.

INT. MEN'S RESTROOM, CYBER JAXX'S - NIGHT

Rob vomits in the toilet.

A QUICK FLASH of Jazz riding shotgun in Rob's car, her hair blowing in the wind, smiling at Rob.

Rob slides to the floor, cups his face, and cries. Uncontrollably. Removes his hands from his face. They're both shaking. His eyes suddenly widen in shock...

INT. INTERNET CAFE, CYBER JAXX'S - NIGHT

Rob rewinds the video to the beginning. Finds the shot where the cameraman answers the door and then presses pause.

ON THE MONITOR

A STILL of a man's hand right before the hand peels back the curtain. Two silver RINGS, one worn on the middle finger and the other worn on the ring finger.

INT. ROB'S HONDA CIVIC - NIGHT

Rob drives past a packed Crystal Palace. The same cruiser is parked in the parking lot. Same two cops seated inside, OFFICER MALONE and OFFICER RODRIQUEZ.

EXT. THE INN MOTEL - NIGHT

Halfway toward the room, Rob pauses from the sight of the cracked door, as well as the lamps turned on inside. He removes the revolver from his belt. Creeps closer.

INT./EXT. MOTEL ROOM, THE INN - NIGHT

Revolver in hand, Rob cautiously opens the door. Surveys the empty room. Not a soul in sight. He suddenly flinches from the sound of the tires SCREECHING behind him!

Rob races outside where Nico's blue Lambo speeds away into the dark night...

INT./EXT. OLD TOWN DINER - NIGHT

Rob sits at the bar, sipping from a cup of coffee. His burner rings. He checks the number. Nico.

> ROB
>
> Hello.

> NICO (V.O.)
> Meet me at Strand Island in half an
> hour.

Rob leaves the diner and walks to his car. He checks the desolate, eerie streets around him. Something's in the air.

INT. ROB'S HONDA CIVIC - CONTINUOUS

Rob closes the door behind him; and as he starts the ignition, we see a glimpse of Moses' ashen face in the mirror on the side of the door...

EXT. STRAND ISLAND - NIGHT

Rob walks to the BEACH where Nico and his friend, YOGI, Yolanda's brother, are standing in a ring of headlights. The other people with Nico remain as dark as shadows, like some sort of death cult circling around their leader.

> ROB
> (nodding at the cars)
> What's this all about, Nico?

Nico doesn't respond; instead, he nods at a black TOWN CAR with tinted windows. Bishop steps out of the car. Walks up to Rob with a queer smirk on his face.

> BISHOP
> (charmingly)
> I'm glad you made it. We have a
> lot to talk about, Mr. Backer.

Rob tightens his jaw, his hand inching closer to the revolver behind his belt.

Suddenly, two men dressed in black -- one of them being Argento -- grab Rob from behind. They throw a black bag over Rob's head. Rob attempts to fight them off, but a swift kick to the bend of his knee causes his legs to give way.

As Rob struggles, Argento fastens his wrists together with a zip tie. Does the same with his ankles. Then, they drag Rob from the beach and toss him inside the back of a van.

> NICO
> What are you doing?

> BISHOP
> I'm doing what's necessary, Nico.

> NICO
> You said he wouldn't be harmed...

> BISHOP
> (sinisterly)
> I lied.

Bishop walks away as the van speeds away.

INT. VAN - NIGHT

As the van brakes, Rob reaches for his revolver but it's nowhere to be found. The rear doors open. An amber street light cuts through the van. Rob squirms. The same two men grab Rob by the ankles and yank him from the van.

EXT. BRIAR CANYON CEMETERY - CONTINUOUS

Argento cuts the zip ties while the other one removes the black bag. Rob frantically looks around. Turns to his left where the barrel of a pistol is being shoved in his face.

> MAN IN BLACK
> Don't even think about it!

The strange men guide Rob to a grave site where a town car is burning its bright headlights over a group of bodyguard-type men, including Bishop, as well as a tall MAN in a black overcoat with his back facing Rob.

A frantic Rob is forced to his knees. He tilts his head upward. The headstone reads: CONRAD ARTIMUS WEST. Next to the grave: a shallow hole. Then, the mysterious man in the black overcoat slowly reveals himself to Rob...

Daniel Ayker!

Gravelly, Ayker pulls his eyes toward the headstone. Runs his gloved hand along the top of the headstone.

> AYKER
>
> Two types of people in this world,
> Mr. Backer: people who go out
> 'looking' for trouble and people who
> go out 'asking' for trouble.

Ayker shoots a glance at Rob, an icy expression.

> AYKER (CONT'D)
>
> I still haven't quite figured out
> which one you are...

One of Ayker's BODYGUARDS hands a revolver to Ayker.

> BODYGUARD
>
> We found this on him.

Ayker studies the red tape wrapped around the handle of the revolver. Lets out a noise under his visible breath, not a moan or a sigh, but somewhere in between. He empties the chamber into his palm. Pockets the bullets, except two, which he inserts inside the chamber.

> AYKER
>
> When Nico first informed me
> about his father, I knew Connie's
> demons had finally caught up with
> him. Then, I heard about a local
> man named Anthony Foster.

Ayker paces around Rob, shaking his head in disgust.

> AYKER (CONT'D)
>
> I knew it couldn't have been a
> coincidence. I couldn't help but
> wonder, 'How would he get to me?'
> Luther finds him snooping around
> his club, going through his personal
> possessions. Is he trying to find
> something to use against Luther? If
> so, for what purpose?

Ayker kneels down in front of Rob.

> AYKER (CONT'D)
> Now that the cards have been laid
> out on the table, why don't you tell
> me? How were you going to bring
> us down, Mr. Backer? I mean,
> really? Amuse me.

Rob doesn't answer. Doesn't do anything, really.

> ROB
> I don't have to explain myself to
> you, you piece of shit!

Rob spits in Ayker's face; in return, he backhands Rob across the face. He wipes
the spit away with a handkerchief from his breast pocket.

> AYKER
> After all these years, Thomas
> Backer's no-good son finally did
> something that his father could
> never do: grow some <u>balls</u>. Or, as
> my business partners say in the
> South: <u>cojones</u>.

The comment stirs a couple of chortles from the others, including Bishop.

> ROB
> (seething)
> You don't know half the shit my
> father's been through...

> AYKER
> (nonchalantly)
> He was weak, Robert. You, on the
> other hand, I remember Luther
> mentioned your name before. You
> and that one hero cop, Arlington.
> Both of you on your little self-
> righteous vendetta. We all knew
> you two weren't a threat. You guys
> had no stomach, no cojones...
> (tilting his head)
> ...Now, well, you filled in to your
> fullest potential. You know,
> Robert, if I knew James's death was
> gonna drive you insane, I would've
> made it a lot easier on you and done
> you myself.

Ayker turns to his left, to the silhouettes circled around the grave.

                    AYKER (CONT'D)
          What do you think, Tony?

A man steps forward in the hazy light. He shares similar features as Anthony
Foster, same height, same weight, same built; however, he's not a twin, not a
double, not a look-alike, not a clone, not even a doppelganger.

                    AYKER (CONT'D)
          I don't believe you two have met.
          Anthony Foster meet James Backer's
          baby brother, Robert.

The man, ANTHONY FOSTER, approaches Rob.

                    ROB
          You're dead.

                    AYKER
          Yes. There was an Anthony Foster
          that did die from an 'apparent'
          heroin overdose; however, not the
          right Anthony Foster, which,
          according to the law, makes you a
          murderer, Mr. Backer.

                    FOSTER
          He's telling the truth.

                    AYKER
          Why don't you tell Mr. Backer here
          about your involvement on the night
          his brother was shot?

Foster hesitates but doesn't answer.

                    AYKER (CONT'D)
          Go on. Tell him...

                    FOSTER
          I was at the club with Bishop while
          Conrad was taking care of some
          personal business outside when
          your...when your brother saw
          something that he shouldn't have.
          Conrad shot him. Not me...
                    (MORE)

>   FOSTER (CONT'D)
>   (pointing at Ayker,
>   Bishop)
>   ...Not Ayker. Not Bishop. I'm
>   sorry for your loss, but your brother
>   was just in the wrong place at the
>   wrong time. That's it --

>   AYKER
>   -- There you go, Mr. Backer.
>   Straight from the horse's mouth.

Ayker stands to his feet, then paces around Rob.

>   ROB
>   If Conrad shot my brother, then
>   why did you arrest the wrong man?

>   AYKER
>   Why? Because I can. That's why.
>   Besides, people like Cedric Gaines
>   are better off behind bars...

Ayker points at the empty grave in front of Rob.

>   ROB
>   (crying)
>   Why Jimmy? Why?

>   AYKER
>   I'm afraid, Mr. Backer, that's just
>   something you have to take up with
>   Conrad...and poor Tony here.

Without delay, Ayker aims the revolver at Foster's belly. Pulls the trigger! BANG!

Foster jolts backward from the sudden gunshot, staggers back and forth. Face long and heavy. Betrayed. Then, Ayker kicks Foster into the empty hole in the earth.

Ayker turns to Rob, snaps close the chamber of the revolver, and tosses it at his feet.

>   AYKER (CONT'D)
>   There you go, Mr. Backer. Happy?

He kneels back down to a speechless Rob.

>   AYKER (CONT'D)
>   And if Luther here sees you in his
>   club ever again...
>   (pointing at the
>   grave)
>   ...you get the point.

He taps Rob on the arm and walks away while the others follow him and walk away as well, including Bishop.

> BISHOP
> (sarcastically)
> Sleep tight, <u>Jimmy</u>.

All of the dark bodies drift away from Rob. Except one. Everybody else gets inside the vans and other cars, but that one remaining person is staring directly at Rob. Eyes like tiny moons. Breathing heavily. Even his cloudy breath is blowing from his nose like the cartoon of an angry bull.

Finally, the last person gets into the back of a car and drives away. Rob picks up the revolver from the ground. The weight is off. He opens the chamber. One bullet inside.

Rob removes the bullet from the chamber and places the bullet in his pocket.

> FOSTER (O.S.)
> (urgently)
> Please! Help me...

Rob looms over Foster, who is curled in a fetal position.

> FOSTER (CONT'D)
> Robert, please! I had nothing to do
> with what happened to your
> brother! You have to believe me --

Rob leaves the cemetery.

> FOSTER (O.S.) (CONT'D)
> Robert! Please don't let me die like
> this! Robert!

EXT. ONE-WAY DINER - NIGHT

As Rob waits in front of a payphone, the TAXI pulls up next to him. Rob steps inside the taxi. Then they ride away.

INT. TAXI - NIGHT

With his head pressed against the glass of the backseat window, Rob stares at the distant skyline of Los Angeles.

EXT. BRIAR CANYON CEMETERY - DAY

Foster's red eyes roll upward, tracing the dark figure looming above. He removes his bloody hand from his stomach and shields the ray of sun. Above him stands Nico. He pulls out the Beretta. Aims the barrel at an exhausted Foster.

>   FOSTER
>   He'll use you the same way he used
>   me. So, go ahead, Nico. Get it
>   over with...

INT. TRUMAN'S GIFT SHOP/GAS STATION - DAY

Rob stands in front of a shelf of Mason jar aquariums and stares at his warped reflection in the glass. He looks down at Jazz's number on his burner.

A QUICK FLASH of Jazz being violated by a burly BLACK MAN wearing a black ski mask.

Rob turns to a younger COUPLE laughing and making out in the book aisle. He scowls. Then turns his narrow eyes back to a Mason jar with a toy scuba diver figurine inside.

INT. MOTEL ROOM, HIGHWAY STAY - DAY

At the doorway, Rob surveys the emptiness all around him.

The filth. The squalor. The only living thing comes from a cockroach scurrying along the baseboard.

QUICK FLASHES - THE NIGHT OF THE SHOOTING

-- Bloody and beaten, James is pulled from the trunk.

-- Then, James's lifeless body is dragged to the bridge.

-- Along the way, James fights off Foster, the right one; and in return, Foster pummels James in the face.

Rob removes James's urn from the bookbag. He FLINGS the urn against the wall, smashing it to pieces. Clouds of gray ash shoot into the air. Ashes rain down and pile over the floor.

He drops to his knees and hysterically searches through the ashes. Bawling. He rakes his ash-covered hands down his soggy face, leaving gray streaks on his face. He wears the ash like a mask. Hangs his head...

A piece of metal glimmering like a nugget of gold within a mound of ashes. He plucks the object from the ash and holds it close to his eyes...

A FRAGMENT of a bullet!

INT. INTERNET CAFE, CYBER JAXX'S - DAY

Rob types in the name of the Fitness Guru, EUGENE RUSSO.

ON THE MONITOR

A flashy website with a buff Eugene standing on the front page, both hands planted on his hips, Superhero-style.

EXT. RUSSO'S MANSION, NEW TOWN - DAY

As Rob stands on the street corner, Eugene skids away in a black Porsche.

EXT. PATIO, NICO'S BEACH HOUSE - NIGHT - FLASHBACK

Rob and Sasha share a cigarette.

> SASHA
> -- She was telling me about this one
> guy she met on Craigslist. Famous
> guy. Eugene Russo. He's on TV
> and everything. She mentioned that
> he was into some freaky shit.

INT. GARAGE, RUSSO'S MANSION - DAY - PRESENT DAY

Rob finds one car that doesn't stand out the most from his collection: a black Infiniti Q50. Swaps out Eugene's plates, "2HOT4U," with a Washington State tag.

EXT. THE PAWNSHOP - DAY

In the back, Rob shows the Russian the score in the trunk of the Infiniti: flat screen TVs with surround sound systems, watches, jewelry, paintings, gold and silver things.

> ROB
> Christmas came early this year.

INT. ROB'S INFINITI - DAY - FLASHBACK SEQUENCE

As Rob camps in a parking lot across from Crystal Palace, he takes photos of a truck, ALPINE TRANSPORTATION, picking up a delivery of cardboard boxes behind the popular nightclub.

INT. HOTEL ROOM, DUNES - NIGHT - PRESENT DAY

Rob tacks the developed photo of Alpine Transportations picking up a delivery from Crystal Palace on the wall. Then, next to the photo, he places another one of Officer Malone and Officer Rodriquez, both keeping lookout.

EXT. THE PLEASURESABER FACTORY, LOS ANGELES - DAY - FLASHBACK SEQUENCE

The delivery man, ROOSTER, unloads boxes on the loading dock.

From a safe distance, Rob snaps photos of Nico shaking hands with Rooster. Closing deals.

INT. HOTEL ROOM, DUNES - NIGHT - PRESENT DAY

Rob tacks a photo of Nico shaking hands with Rooster on the wall. He tacks a printout of the already "dead" Anthony Foster next to Nico. Marks a black X over his face.

EXT. THE DOCKS - DAY - FLASHBACK SEQUENCE

Nico is walking with Ayker toward a villainous yacht, several of Ayker's bodyguards keeping their distance.

INT. HOTEL ROOM, DUNES - NIGHT - PRESENT DAY

Rob tacks a photo of both Nico and Ayker on the wall.

EXT. SHIPYARD, HILLSIDE - DAY - FLASHBACK SEQUENCE

Bishop hands Ayker an envelope. They shake hands.

INT. HOTEL ROOM, DUNES - NIGHT - PRESENT DAY

Dragging from a cigarette, Rob tacks another photo of Bishop and Ayker at the shipyard.

Then, he snips off a piece of red yarn and connects all of the photos together: the Alpine truck picking up a delivery to the truck dropping off packages to Nico and Ayker acting chummy at the Docks to Bishop and Ayker doing shady deals.

Next, Rob tacks a photo of Bishop exiting Crystal Palace with the black bear-like bouncer, DARIUS, at the top of his chart.

INT. SMOKIN' JOE'S COFFEE SHOP - NIGHT - FLASHBACK
SEQUENCE

From Rob's new laptop, he watches a video from FORCED ENTRY. He pauses
the video for a closer look. Leans in. Closely.

ON THE MONITOR

A STILL of a well-built black man in a ski mask on top of Jazz. Holding down
the CONTROL key, Rob ZOOMS in on the black man's neck, a tattoo of a
diamond.

EXT. CRYSTAL PALACE - NIGHT - FLASHBACK SEQUENCE

Rob throws his head in a nod at Darius as he and Flip enter the nightclub. Rob's
eyes cross the TATTOO of a diamond on the side of the bouncer's neck...

INT. HOTEL ROOM, DUNES - NIGHT - PRESENT DAY

Rob tacks a photo of Darius on the wall. Then he tacks a photo of Yogi right
next to Darius.

INT. SMOKIN' JOE'S COFFEE SHOP - NIGHT - FLASHBACK
SEQUENCE

Rob rewinds the video. Pauses the video.

ON THE MONITOR

A heavyset Latino man wearing a ski mask looms over Jazz as she gives him a
blowjob. Rob ZOOMS IN on a mole in the shape of Texas underneath his left
breast.

INT. INTERNET CAFE, CYBER JAXX'S - DAY - FLASHBACK SEQUENCE

Rob scrolls through Yogi's Instagram page.

ON THE MONITOR

A photo of Yogi and his sister, Yolanda, at New Town Beach. The same Texas-
shaped mole underneath Yogi's left breast.

INT. HOTEL ROOM, DUNES - NIGHT - PRESENT DAY

Next to Yogi, Rob tacks a CLOSE UP of Ayker's grainy face taken from the TV screen on the wall.

Then, he tacks two cutouts from old newspapers: one of handcuffed "Cedric Gaines," then the other of "Henry Frick's skeleton" being pulled from the river.

Next to these two articles, he tacks a Polaroid of Henry and his sister, "BELLA," then Conrad's missing wife, "MYRTLE."

Lastly, Rob grabs a photo of Jazz from his pile of photos. The one from her purse, of a younger, much heavier Jazz. He hangs James's gold necklace over the tack.

Rob admires all of the photos and newspaper clippings covering the entire wall. His own wall of suspects and victims. Pinned and mounted. He hones in on the incumbent sheriff of Los Angeles County, Daniel Ayker...

INT. TOWN CAR - NIGHT

Nico takes a seat across from a pensive Ayker.

> NICO
> He's currently staying at some
> crummy hotel off Walker Avenue.
> Hardly leaves the room during the
> day. Spends his nights at bars. I
> think he got the picture.

> AYKER
> How sure are you?

> NICO
> He <u>won't</u> be a problem anymore.

Ayker turns his attention back to the window.

> AYKER
> (quietly)
> Good, Nico. Very good.

INT. CYBER JAXX'S - DAY

Ruby approaches the MANAGER with his badge already on display. Then, he shows him a photo of MOSES.

> RUBY
> Have you seen this man before?

81

INT. FANBOY'S VIDEO STORE - DAY

Rob browses through the thriller aisle. He passes Martin Scorsese's "TAXI DRIVER." Skims the back summary of the DVD.

INT. CYBER JAXX'S - DAY

Ruby searches through the SEARCH HISTORY. Finds several links to a vacationing spot called "SHIES LODGE."

INT. HOTEL ROOM, DUNES - NIGHT

Rob watches the scene where Robert De Niro's character assembles a special contraption along his wrist. He takes notes as well as sketches designs in a notebook.

INT. CHUCK'S HARDWARE STORE - DAY

Rob picks up a metal track from the shelf. Examines the width and length. Buys the necessary supplies.

INT. HOTEL ROOM, DUNES - DAY

Over the table, Rob saws the track to the length of his forearm. Places the track along his arm.

EXT. TOPSIDE BEACH - DAY

Rob jogs along the shore, stops, and checks his pulse. Counts. Then catches his breath and keeps running.

EXT. ALLEYWAY, OLD TOWN - NIGHT

A GUN DEALER opens the case for Rob. Inside is a Beretta PX4 Storm Subcompact. Rob pays for the handgun with cash.

INT. BATHROOM, HOTEL ROOM - NIGHT

In front of the mirror, Rob attaches the finished contraption over his right forearm. Locks the Beretta Storm inside the holder along the track. Flicks back his wrist, causing the Beretta to slide into his hand!

INT. HOTEL ROOM, DUNES - DAY

Rob places the keychain with the rabbit's foot and the key to his chest, as well as a personally handwritten letter inside the envelope. Then, he writes "John Ruby" on the front.

EXT. POST OFFICE - DAY

Rob parks next to the mailbox and drops the envelope inside.

INT. SUNDAY'S BEST, MEN'S CLOTHING STORE - DAY

Dressed in Johnny Cash-black, Rob stands in front of the dressing room mirror. He glances down at his right sleeve.

INT. LINES AND LINENS - DAY

Rob stands in front of a shower curtain with magnets on display. He opens and closes the curtain. The magnets lock the curtain together. It's perfect.

INT. BATHROOM, HOTEL ROOM - NIGHT

Rob cuts through the right sleeve with scissors, then hot glues the magnets onto the flaps of the inner sleeve. He releases the Beretta from the contraption. The sleeve opens smoothly. Locks the handgun back into place. The sleeve closes, like the shower curtain, by magnetization.

> MOSES (O.S.)
> (faintly)
> Are you forgetting something?

Rob turns to the corner of the room.

INT. HOTEL ROOM, DUNES - CONTINUOUS

Rob exits the bathroom. A lamp shines on the emaciated body of Moses seated in a chair. He's dressed in a black suit. His skin is grayish in color. Corpse-like.

> ROB
> I don't have time to be doing any
> 'favors' right now.

Moses coughs, a phlegmy one.

> MOSES
> You'll have time.

Rob grabs the sealed ice bucket -- James's urn -- from the dresser and heads toward the door.

> MOSES (O.S.) (CONT'D)
> What if I were to tell you that you
> could have your life back, without
> regrets, without anger...

Moses stands up. His posture, weaker than before. Part of his skeletal face is exposed in the dim light.

> MOSES (CONT'D)
> ...without me.

Rob turns around. Faces Moses.

> ROB
> Almost sounds too good to be true.

> MOSES
> There's a man, Fran Rosalie. He
> has something that belongs to me.

> ROB
> (sourly)
> Get it yourself.

> MOSES
> No. It must be you.

INT. ROB'S INFINITI - CONTINUOUS

Rob cuts the headlights as he pulls into the TRAILER PARK. In the backseat sits a decrepit-looking Moses. Rob looks in the rear view mirror. Repulsed.

> ROB
> You don't look too good...

> MOSES
> (coughing)
> I'll live.

EXT. ROSALIE'S TRAILER - NIGHT

Rob sneaks to the window where Fran's downing the rest of his canned beer. Fran burps, propels out of the holey recliner, and scratches his ass while walking to the bathroom.

INT. ROSALIE'S TRAILER - NIGHT

Rob gently closes the door behind him. He creeps to Ivory's case, which is settled on top of a shelf housing other strange objects, including two-headed frogs and a dead fetus with horns inside of a jar.

A FLUSH of a toilet startles Rob!

> FRAN (O.S.)
> Hey! What the hell are you doing?

Rob bolts from the trailer.

EXT. ROSALIE'S TRAILER - CONTINUOUS

Fran chases after Rob but Rob is too fast for him.

> FRAN
> Get back here!
> (kicking the dirt)
> Goddamn it...

EXT. ABANDONED PARKING LOT - NIGHT

As Rob towers over an oil drum, he tosses the magazines from his bookbag into the fire. The smut material. The DVD.

Lastly, Rob places Ivory's head in the fire. Flames rip through the first layer of her skin, then peel away a partially torn brownish tag with a BARCODE behind _its_ ear!

The reflection of flames RISE inside Rob's glossy eyes...

MONTAGE -- ROB'S BLOODY REVENGE

-- INT. YOGI'S BEDROOM - NIGHT -- Rob steps out of the closet and shoots Yogi. Two shots in the chest. One in the head.

-- INT. YOGI'S LIVING ROOM - NIGHT -- Rob sets Yogi's furniture on fire with a can of gasoline and a Zippo lighter.

-- EXT. YOGI'S HOUSE - NIGHT -- Rob strides like a badass from the flaming house. Doesn't look back. Badass.

-- EXT. PARKING LOT - NIGHT -- Rob anxiously waits for the cops to receive the dispatch, urges them to leave.

INT. POLICE CRUISER - CONTINUOUS

Officer Rodriquez receives the dispatch. A fire. He turns to partner, answers the dispatcher.

> RODRIQUEZ
> We're on our way.

EXT. PARKING LOT - CONTINUOUS

Rob watches the cruiser flip on its sirens, then peel away.

EXT. FRONT ENTRANCE, CRYSTAL PALACE - CONTINUOUS

Rob storms toward the bouncer, Darius. The Beretta concealed underneath his sleeve. Darius extends his arm outward, his mitt of a hand motioning for Rob to stop in his tracks.

The Beretta shoots from the edge of Rob's sleeve. Rob places the barrel to Darius's chest. Pulls the trigger. His eyes glow like tiny ambers as the smoke slithers from his mouth.

The other bouncer, Zeek, charges from the entrance. Rob SHOOTS Zeek in the kneecap, forcing him to the ground.

INT. CRYSTAL PALACE - NIGHT

Rob prowls through crowds, most of the clubbers unaware of the gunshots outside since the beat of the dark witch house music itself sounds like gunshots.

The guards stationed around the nightclub touch the earpiece in their ears, then rush from their posts and search the crowds; however, the two men guarding the stairs, GUARD #3 and GUARD #4, don't budge an inch.

> GUARD #1
> Got 'em...

On the DANCE FLOOR, Flip and Drew dance with a couple of girls, Drew wearing a different colored cast on his arm.

As the other guards guide the clubbers from the club, GUARD #1 rushes toward Rob. Ready to pounce on Rob.

A hand grabs Rob by the shoulder. He spins around. Flip.

> FLIP
> Hey, muthafucka. You gotta lot of
> fuckin' nerve showin' up here...

Guard #1 closes in on Rob!

Flip grabs Rob yet again. Rob bends back four of the five fingers on Flip's hand, dislocating them. Flip retaliates by throwing a wild punch.

Rob dodges Flip's Hail Mary swing and counters with a spit of a jab directly to his jugular; temporarily incapacitates him.

As Rob spins around, Guard #1 is rearing back the blackjack in his hand. Rob reacts by removing the butterfly knife from his belt and stabs the guard in the forearm. The blackjack falls from his grip. Rob removes the blade.

In one fluid motion, he does a Michael Jackson-like twirl on the slick dance floor and slices the guard across his gut.

GUARD #2 pushes frantic bodies away and removes a handgun from underneath his blazer. The Beretta springs from Rob's wrist. Into Rob's hand. He shoots Guard #2 in the shoulder.

A once even-tempered crowd now turns into a full-on stampede toward the EXIT after the blast of the gunshot!

Rob breaks away from the frenzied crowd, seeks out Guard #3 and Guard #4 below the staircase, BLASTS them away.

INT. SECOND FLOOR, CRYSTAL PALACE - CONTINUOUS

Rob slides another magazine into the Beretta as he makes his way up the stairs. Checks the SURVEILLANCE ROOM first.

INT. SURVELLIANCE ROOM, CRYSTAL PALACE - CONTINUOUS

As Rob checks the monitors, a shadowy figure creeps from behind the doorway...

A CREAK in the floor!

Rob rotates, only to be jolted backward from a blade being thrust into the back of his shoulder. The Beretta springs from Rob's wrist; however, Argento kicks the handgun from the contraption, causing it to skip along the floor. He removes the blade from his back.

Then Argento lunges at Rob. Punches Rob across the face, dazing him. Rob tackles Argento. They both CRASH through a table! Glass everywhere.

The two wrestle around: Rob bites Argento in the neck; Argento returns with an elbow to Rob's face; then, Rob, dazed, crawls to the Beretta. Crawling. Fingering.

As Rob gets a finger on the handle, the butt of a fire extinguisher CRUSHES his left hand, breaking several fingers.

Then, Argento straddles Rob and goes to town. Rob RETRACTS the contraption. Grabs Argento by the collar. Extends his wrist backward, releasing the empty track from his wrist...

The track PENETRATES Argento's throat. He's bleeding, profusely. Panic washes over his face as he stumbles away, trying to find something to cover the wound.

Rob picks up the Beretta and locks it in its rightful place.

Argento falls to the floor from the substantial loss of blood. Rob looms over the dying man. He lets him bleed out.

INT. SECOND FLOOR, CRYSTAL PALACE - CONTINUOUS

Rob evaluates his injuries: first, his hand. His fingers are as crooked as an arthritic hand. He runs his other hand over his left shoulder blade. Removes a handful of blood.

> JAZZ (O.S.)
>> (groaning)
> Get off me...

Rob rushes to Jazz's muffled voice coming from a closed door at the end of the hallway. Presses his ear against the door.

> JAZZ (O.S.) (CONT'D)
>> (crying)
> Stop! Please! Help me...

Stricken with rage, Rob races to a box on the wall. Inside the box: the reel of a fire hose, as well as a red axe with a wooden handle. He goes with the axe.

INT. YELLOW ROOM, SECOND FLOOR - NIGHT

Rob slinks through the curtain, axe gripped in one hand and the fire extinguisher held in the other. Surveys the damage to the room: a round hole in the shape of a head in the wall; an overturn couch; a can of pepper spray on the floor; the orange liquid sprayed over the floor as well as the wall.

Across the room, Jazz's hands are tied to the handle of the desk's drawers. Naked. Bruised. Bloody. Raped.

Behind Jazz stoops a man with his slacks cuffed around his ankles. The man's fucking Jazz, violently. The sleeves of his sports coat are wrapped around Jazz's throat, and he uses the coat to strangle her. Rob spins the man around...

Bishop!

Rob kicks Bishop in his knee, forcing him to the floor.

> ROB
> You like choking women...

He pries open Bishop's mouth, turns the axe upside down, handle side first.

> ROB (CONT'D)
> Choke on this, motherfucker!

Rob JAMS the handle down his throat. Bishop resists by grabbing at the axe, but Rob SLAMS the heel of his foot into his crotch. He slides the handle halfway down his esophagus, takes the butt of the fire extinguisher, and RAMS it into the handle, snapping it in half. Part of the handle protrudes from the side of Bishop's neck but never pierces the skin.

Only a couple of seconds pass before Bishop collapses to the floor, the frothy blood streaming from his nose and the corners of his mouth. Dead.

Rob unties Jazz from the desk. She staggers. Her hands cupping her bloody groin. Rob holds Jazz in his arms. She's crying. So ashamed that she can hardly look Rob in the eyes.

> ROB (CONT'D)
> You're safe now...

Behind Rob and Jazz a concealed CAMERA mounted on a tripod films the entire scene. The red light, glowing strong.

INT. DANCE FLOOR, CRYSTAL PALACE - NIGHT

Rob points toward the green EXIT sign above the kitchen.

> ROB
> Meet me at the Galatia.

> JAZZ
> What are you gonna do?

Rob turns to the secret room, the one with the RED door.

> ROB
> I need to take care of some business.

Jazz doesn't move an inch. She's crying. Rob hugs her.

ROB (CONT'D)
Everything's going to be fine. Now
go. I'm right behind you...

Jazz leaves the club.

INT. RED ROOM, CRYSTAL PALACE - NIGHT

Rob shoots off the lock, then kick's open the door!

Rows and rows of tables are lined in the center of the room. Along the walls are stacks of cardboard boxes.

Rob runs his finger over the powdery residue along the table's surface. Samples a taste. Cocaine. He walks over to the boxes.

The sides of each box reads, "THE PLEASURESABER^{TM}."

Rob pulls out one of Nico's sex toys from the box, then he pulls out an eightball of cocaine from inside the sleeve.

NICO (O.S.)
Robert!

Rob drops the sex toy, then the drugs. Rotates around. Nico's pointing a gun at Rob.

ROB
Nico? What are you doing here?

Nico's eyes draw down toward Rob's left hand.

NICO
What did you do?

ROB
I did what I had to do.

Nico aims the barrel at Rob's head.

NICO
You're not going anywhere.

ROB
You're not going to shoot me,
Nico.

NICO
Oh yeah! Why the fuck not?

ROB
It's not who you are...

                    NICO
        You don't know a thing about me --

                    ROB
        -- I know you're <u>not</u> a killer.

As police sirens WAIL from outside, Rob slips past Nico.

                    NICO (O.S.)
        Ayker! It was Ayker...

Rob stops in his tracks. Faces Nico.

                    NICO (CONT'D)
        ...Ayker was the one who shot your
        brother. Not my father.

Rob remains in a state of bafflement.

                    NICO (CONT'D)
        Ayker told me all about it. He said
        your brother witnessed a murder.
        He shot him. Left him to die, but
        he didn't die. Did he?

                    ROB
        No. He didn't.

Rob walks away.

                    NICO (O.S.)
        They'll kill you! Is that what you
        want?

INT. KITCHEN, CRYSTAL PALACE - CONTINUOUS

Rob passes a gas line. Improvises by grabbing a bottle of vodka from the top shelf.
Dowses a rag with vodka and stuffs the damp rag into the half full bottle of liquor.
He places the bottle over the stovetop, turns the knob to the highest setting, and
lights the rag on fire with a torch.

Then, lastly, Rob YANKS the gas line from the wall and exits through the back
door.

EXT. CRYSTAL PALACE - NIGHT

As Rob walks through the parking lot, the club erupts in a ball of flames behind him.

INT. ROB'S INFINITI - NIGHT

Rob drives past a fleet of fire trucks and police cruisers.

EXT./INT. THE GALATIA - NIGHT

Rob searches for Jazz, but Jazz is nowhere in sight. He checks the ARCADE, the BATHROOMS. He calls Jazz but her phone is going straight to voicemail.

As Rob makes his way to the front of the building, two cops approach the arcade. Checking ID's and questioning kids. Rob decides to dip without Jazz.

INT. ROB'S INFINITI - NIGHT

Rob does an abrupt U-turn, several cars blowing their horns.

EXT. CRYSTAL PALACE - NIGHT

Rob drives past the club, swarming with cops, fire fighters, and NEWS vans. One side of the club is covered in flames. Again, Jazz is nowhere in sight!

EXT. DRIVEWAY, NEIGHBORHOOD - NIGHT

Rob removes his belongings from the car. He breaks into a Volvo wagon, puts his belongings inside, and drives away.

INT. ROB'S VOLVO - NIGHT

Rob passes the sign for BRIAR CANYON. Calls Jazz along the way. No answer. Again. He stops at a Luxury Suites Motel on the side of the highway. Disguises himself with a baseball cap that he finds in the back of the wagon.

EXT./INT. LUXURY SUITES - CONTINUOUS

Rob walks into the lobby. Places a wad of bloody cash on the counter before the DESK CLERK.

                    ROB
        I need a room.

INT. BATHROOM, MOTEL ROOM - NIGHT

Rob grabs the gauze from the first-aid kit and places it over the stab wound on his back. Then, he straightens the bones in his fingers, aligns them, and makes a splint with a couple of pens as well as a piece of lining from a bed sheet.

INT. MOTEL ROOM, LUXURY SUITES - NIGHT

Rob turns on the TV and flips through NEWS channels.

ON THE SCREEN

Footage of a burning Crystal Palace, the headline below: "SHOOTING AT PRIVATE NIGHTCLUB, MANY DEAD."

BACK IN THE ROOM

The burner suddenly RINGS in Rob's pocket. He checks the number. It's Jazz's number! Rob answers.

> ROB
> (out of breath)
> Jazz! Where are you?

INT. AYKER'S TOWN CAR - CONTINUOUS

Ayker smirks.

> AYKER
> I'm sorry, Mr. Backer. Jazz is all
> tied up at the moment. Would you
> like for me to take a message?

He turns to Jazz seated next to him. Duct tape over her mouth. Wrists taped. A shiner on the left side of her face.

INTERCUT - TELEPHONE CONVERSATION

> ROB
> Where is she?

> AYKER
> You should've taken my advice
> when you had the chance, Mr.
> Backer.

> ROB
> (fuming)
> Where is she!

Ayker places the phone next to Jazz's mouth and peels away part of the tape.

                          JAZZ
            Get outta there! He's gonna --

INT. MOTEL ROOM, LUXURY SUITES - CONTINUOUS

Jazz SQUEALS over the other end...

                          ROB
            Jazz?

The phone cuts off for a second, then a THUD rattles the phone's receiver!

                          AYKER (V.O.)
            Now, do I have your attention?

                          ROB
            Just let her go, and I'll do whatever
            you want...

Rob walks to the window and peeks out the curtain.

                          AYKER
            I'm afraid it's not that simple.

Rob turns around and draws his attention toward the TV.

ON THE SCREEN

Footage of Moses on a surveillance camera inside the video store, FANBOY'S, purchasing a DVD at the checkout counter. The frame STILLS and then ZOOMS in on his face.

BACK TO ROB

who furrows his brows in confusion.

                          AYKER (V.O.) (CONT'D)
            Are you there?

                          ROB
            What do you want from me?

                          AYKER (V.O.)
            What do I want? I want you to
            disappear...

                          ROB
            Deal. You'll never hear from me
            ever again. Let her go. Please --

> AYKER
> -- You know, Mr. Backer, you
> remind me a lot of Henry, a young
> man who bit off more than he
> could chew. I bet you didn't know
> this but after I took care of poor
> Henry, Myrtle went back to
> Connie. And he didn't even love
> the woman, yet the very night she
> shot that son of a bitch in the face,
> he was on his knees, begging for her
> to take him back. A grown man
> <u>begging</u>. Can you believe that?

INT. AYKER'S TOWN CAR - CONTINUOUS

Ayker runs his fingers over the side of Jazz's bloody face.

> AYKER (O.S.)
> I swear people will say the craziest
> things when they're staring at the
> face of death...

INT. MOTEL ROOM, LUXURY SUITES - CONTINUOUS

The HORN of a train echoes through the phone. Then, the horn lets out a
WAIL outside the window. A short delay.

Rob rushes back to the window. Peeks outside. There, across a dark field, a
TRAIN passes along the Pacific Coast.

> AYKER (V.O.)
> ...If you want to see your friend ever
> again meet me at the Briar Canyon
> Cemetery in exactly one hour.

Ayker hangs up the phone. Rob flips open the burner and dials a 9 and a 1 and
then stops, thinks. Closes the phone.

INT. BATHROOM, MOTEL ROOM - CONTINUOUS

Grimacing in agony, Rob slithers through the bathroom window.

EXT. LUXURY SUITES - CONTINUOUS

Rob pokes his head around the corner.

Parked about a quarter of a mile away is a black unmarked TOWN CAR, sitting alone in the middle of an open field, the Pacific at its back.

INT. AYKER'S TOWN CAR - CONTINUOUS

Ayker hands the phone to the bodyguard sitting next to him.

> AYKER
> Wait till he leaves, then kill him.

> BODYGUARD
> And what do you want me to do
> with his body?

> AYKER
> Use your imagination.

EXT. VACANT LOT - CONTINUOUS

Rob flanks the town car. Four figures inside the car: two in the front and two in the back.

Rob ducks behind a boulder and checks the revolver's chamber. The haunting sounds of the pump action from a SHOTGUN reverberate over his shoulder...

> BODYGUARD #1 (O.S.)
> Freeze, asshole!

Rob freezes.

BODYGUARD #1 motions for Rob to stand. Rob stands. The bodyguard pats down each one of Rob's pockets. Finds a butterfly knife behind his back. Pockets the knife.

As Bodyguard #1 turns Rob around, the Beretta springs from Rob's wrist. Rob shoots him in the face. He dies instantly.

The passenger door swings open. Another man steps from the car. Gun drawn. Rob unloads on BODYGUARD #2. Hits him in the shoulder. However, the contraption breaks from the last gunshot. Part of metal digs into Rob's flesh, cutting him.

As Rob struggles to remove the contraption, a fight breaks out between the two figures in the backseat. The back door opens, then Jazz stumbles to the ground, kicking around dirt, her arms flailing around.

Rob removes the broken contraption, picks up the shotgun from the ground, and shoots out the driver's window.

> ROB
> (prowling to the car)
> Get outta here!

In the backseat, a GLINT from the distant floodlight glares over a pistol aimed directly at Jazz!

> ROB (CONT'D)
> Get down!

Rob shoots out the back window of the car.

> ROB (CONT'D)
> Run, goddamn it!

Jazz darts toward the beach while Rob shoots at the car. No movement inside the car until...

The driver's door SQUEAKS open and the DRIVER, bloody and slumped over the steering wheel, is pushed out of the car.

The driver's not moving. Possibly dead.

Ayker crawls over the center console of the car, takes the wheel, and then peels away into the night.

Rob grabs his butterfly knife from the dead bodyguard. He checks the driver's pulse. Dead. He approaches Bodyguard #2 slithering away. Rob steps on his back. Flips him around.

> BODYGUARD #2
> (holding out his
> hands)
> Please! Don't kill me...

Rob holds the knife against his throat.

> ROB
> Give me a reason not to --

> BODYGUARD #2
> -- I have a son!

> ROB
> Oh yeah! Then, what the fuck are
> you doing here?

The bodyguard coughs, causing a string of blood to trickle from the side of his mouth.

Rob pulls the blade away. Then takes his weapons: a Glock 19 laying inches away from his hand and then a Beretta 3032 Tomcat from his ankle holster.

EXT. BEACH, HILL'S END - CONTINUOUS

Jazz is pacing around the shore. Worried. She turns her shoulder. Rob's standing on top of a dune. Jazz falls to her knees. Relieved. Rob sits next to her and comforts her.

> ROB
> He's gone.

She buries her head into Rob's shoulder and cries.

> JAZZ
> What do we do now?

> ROB
> We keep moving.

EXT. REDWOODS NATIONAL PARK - DAY

Rob drives down a dirt road surrounded by redwoods as tall as skyscrapers.

INT. ROB'S VOLVO - CONTINUOUS

Rob and Jazz soak up the pleasant view of the redwoods. Jazz cranes her head above the headrest of the passenger seat and stares at Rob's shoulder. Something's not right.

> ROB
> What is it?

Jazz pulls back the collar of his shirt, examines his back, then peels away a piece of dry skin. She shows Rob the skin before she flicks it out the window. She examines some more.

> JAZZ
> Your hurt...
> (touching the
> wound)
> ...It'll get infected.

> ROB
> We just need to keep our heads
> down for a while, then I'll worry --

> JAZZ
> -- Why did you lie about your
> name?

> ROB
> Jimmy was my brother.

> JAZZ
> What happened to him?

Rob doesn't answer, at first.

> JAZZ (CONT'D)
> Sorry. It's none of my business.

Rob sighs, then removes the driver's license from his pocket. Peels his photo from Henry's license. Shaves away the residue from the dry glue with his fingernail.

Rob turns to Jazz, teary-eyed.

> ROB
> They shot him.

> JAZZ
> Why?

> ROB
> He saw something that he wasn't
> supposed to see. That's why.

Jazz grabs Rob's hand, leans over, and hugs him.

INT. BEDROOM, SAFE HOUSE - DAY

With one half of his badly disfigured face highlighted in the glow of the TV, Ayker stares at the STILL of Moses' face.

> ANCHOR (ON TV)
> -- The unidentified white male is
> said to be armed and dangerous. If
> you have seen this man, please
> contact authorities immediately.

EXT. PARKING LOT, STRIP MALL - CONTINUOUS

Jazz places her hand over Rob's forehead.

>   JAZZ
> Robert, you're burning up.

>   ROB
>   (shivering)
> I'm fine. We just need to keep
> movin' --

>   JAZZ
> -- Lemme drive.

INT. ROB'S VOLVO - DAY

As Rob waits in the passenger seat, Jazz returns with a bagful of medicinal supplies.

Rob glances in the rear view mirror. Jazz secretly pockets one of the items inside the bag.

EXT. SHIES LODGE - DAY

Jazz steps out of the Volvo. Rents a cabin for the night.

INT. BATHROOM, CABIN - DAY

Jazz wipes away the dried blood caked over Rob's skin, cleans the wound with sterile soap and water, dries his shoulder with a sterile cloth, then carefully rubs the gel from a broken Aloe leaf over the wound.

>   ROB
> You would've made a great nurse.

>   JAZZ
> I thought about it once, but I don't
> know if I could handle the sight of
> blood.

>   ROB
>   (carelessly)
> You would've fooled me.

>   JAZZ
> This, I can handle.

Jazz places a dressing over Rob's shoulder. Rob grabs Jazz by the wrist while she applies the last piece of tape.

> ROB
> You don't have to be here.

> JAZZ
> I'm not leaving you --

> ROB
> -- You'll be an accessory.

> JAZZ
> Maybe...
> > (leaning in closer)
> ...I'll just tell them you kidnapped me.

> ROB
> You wouldn't.

> JAZZ
> No, but I won't have to. Right?

> ROB
> Right.

INT. CABIN, SHIES LODGE - NIGHT

Rob goes through Jazz's phone. Scrolls through selfies until he comes across a photo of Jazz standing with Moses.

ON THE PHONE

Outside Blue Lounge poses Moses and Jazz, his arm wrapped around her waist, both of them smiling like two cats.

BACK TO ROB

who scrolls through more photos of Jazz and Moses taken on the boardwalk, photos of them drinking at a bar, photos of them at the Freakspectacular show, photos of them kissing.

The SHOWER turns off.

Rob slips back into bed as Jazz steps from the bathroom. She directs her attention toward the TV where the same clip's replaying over and over: Moses entering Crystal Palace with his gun drawn. He grabs the remote and turns up the volume.

ON THE SCREEN

Below the grainy black and white STILL of Moses, the headline reads: MASSIVE DRUG RING EXPOSED, TIED TO POLICE CORRUPTION.

> ANCHOR (ON TV)
> Suspect has been identified as thirty-one-year-old Robert Backer from Charlotte, North Carolina. Mr. Backer originally grew up in the Los Angeles area, then moved to the Carolinas in his early teens.

BACK TO JAZZ

who sits on the bed next to a stunned Rob.

> LAWYER (ON TV)
> Two years ago Backer was admitted to Red Pines, a mental institution located in the Appalachian Mountains, for assaulting a man outside a bar in the small town of Cullowhee.

A QUICK FLASH of an unhinged Rob towering like a giant over a badly injured man, DALE ROLLINS, 20's, outside the sleazy Bull Pigeons Bar -- both of Rob's tightly coiled fists dripping with fresh blood.

The remote slips from Rob's grip and lands on the floor.

INT. RECREATIONAL ROOM, RED PINES - NIGHT - FLASHBACK SEQUENCE

Rob watches the film, "SEVEN SAMURAI." Across the room sits Moses. Rob turns his head toward Moses. In return, Moses squares himself to Rob. They both acknowledge each other.

INT. CABIN, SHIES LODGE - NIGHT - PRESENT DAY

Rob suddenly rushes to the bathroom.

> JAZZ
> Robert? Are you okay?

Jazz follows.

INT. BATHROOM, CABIN - CONTINUOUS

Rob closes the door. Vomits in toilet. A TAP on the door!

                              JAZZ (O.S.)
          Can I come in?

                              ROB
          Just a minute!

Rob flushes the toilet and picks up a pregnancy test in the trash can. Reads the POSITIVE sign. He faces the mirror.

Then, he feverishly scratches the flesh a his face. The itch grows deeper, his skin loosens. His fingertips dig underneath his flesh. He claws and tears sheets of flesh from his face. He ends up ripping off his entire face!

Rob stares at the pile of flesh in the sink, then turns his wide eyes upward at the reflection. Runs his coarse hands along the hard stubs on his cheeks, the five o'clock shadow. He pulls his hands away from his face -- Moses' face!

INT. CABIN, SHIES LODGE - CONTINUOUS

As Rob eases from the bathroom, Jazz is sitting on the edge of the bed. She appears worried again.

                              JAZZ
          You look a little pale.

Rob sits down next to Jazz. Hangs his head.

                              ROB
                    (quietly)
          When I was a kid, they used to call
          me Moe. Short for Moses.

                              JAZZ
          Robert, are you okay?

                              ROB
          I used to make these predictions all
          the time and then, whenever they
          came true, I'd tell them, 'I told you
          so,' as if I was rubbing it in their
          faces, but I really wasn't. They
          didn't like that, me being right and
          them wrong.

Rob faces Jazz. Worried as well.

                              ROB (CONT'D)
          I don't know what's going to
          happen to us.

                              103

Jazz slides her hand over his knee. They interlock hands.

> ROB (CONT'D)
> I'm scared.

> JAZZ
> Me too.

EXT. WOODS - NIGHT - DREAM (THE LAW CLOSING IN)

A FBI AGENT motions to dozens of agents stalking around the trees, toward the lit cabin, assault rifles ready to fire.

INT. CABIN, SHIES LODGE - DAY - PRESENT DAY

Rob wakes from a door opening. Rays of sunlight hit Rob in the face, then Jazz strolls inside, carrying a cardboard holder with two cups of coffee and a couple of pastries.

> JAZZ
> Did you sleep well?

> ROB
> (rubbing his eyes)
> So-so.

EXT./INT. CABIN, SHIES LODGE - DAY

Jazz cuts firewood with an axe. She sets axe aside as Rob watches her from the window. She grabs an armful of the firewood and returns back to the cabin where Rob's packing his bookbag.

> JAZZ
> (surprised)
> Where are you going?

> ROB
> (packing James's
> urn)
> There's one last thing I need to take care of.

Jazz sets aside the firewood.

> JAZZ
> You think that's a good idea right
> now, with everything that's
> happening?

> ROB
> Maybe not, but it's something I
> <u>need</u> to do.

Rob places one-strap of the bookbag over his shoulder.

> JAZZ
> What if they find you?

> ROB
> They won't.

> JAZZ
> I can't do this alone, Robert!

> ROB
> They <u>won't</u> find me!

Rob calms his breathing. Approaches a frightened Jazz.

> ROB (CONT'D)
> I'm sorry...
> (closely)
> ...I'll be right back. I promise.

He kisses Jazz on the cheek, then leaves.

EXT. SHIES LODGE - CONTINUOUS

Rob drives away. He blindly passes a parked car with Ruby seated in the driver's seat. Ruby pulls out his phone.

INT. BACKER'S RESIDENCE - DAY

Susannah picks up the telephone.

> SUSANNAH
> Hello.

INT. RUBY'S CAR - CONTINUOUS

Ruby closely watches Rob drive away.

> RUBY
> Susannah. It's John. I found him.

INT. BEDROOM, BACKER'S RESIDENCE - DAY

Thomas rushes from the closet to the bed, packing his bag while, at the same time, Susannah's crying.

> SUSANNAH
> Thomas, please! Bring him back!
> Don't let anything happen to my
> boy!

Thomas grabs his wife, consoles her.

> THOMAS
> Everything's going to be okay. I
> promise.

EXT. NORTH CREEK BEACH - NIGHT

As the red sun sets, Rob kicks off his shoes and takes the urn to a calm sea. Removes the tape from the bucket.

> ROB
> Goodbye, Jimmy.

Rob dumps James's ashes into the sea.

EXT. BEACH ACCESS, NORTH CREEK BEACH - NIGHT

Rob passes a PEDESTRIAN, 70's, stepping out of a red smart car. She nods hello at Rob. Then does a double take.

EXT./INT. SHIES LODGE - NIGHT

As Rob skids to a stop, the spotlight of a HELICOPTER cuts across the black sky. He races inside the cabin. Jazz is watching a "BREAKING REPORT" on TV, chewing her nails.

> ROB
> We have to leave now!

ON THE SCREEN

An OVERHEAD shot from the helicopter showing Rob weaving in and out of traffic with two cruisers close on his tail.

BACK TO JAZZ

who turns to Rob with a sense of defeat on her face.

> JAZZ
> What happened?

> ROB
> I don't have time to explain.

Rob collects all of Jazz's things, as well as his weapons.

> ROB (CONT'D)
> We'll keep driving north until we
> reach the border.

> JAZZ
> They won't stop, Robert!

Jazz flips through the NEWS channels: Faces of Moses everywhere.

> JAZZ (CONT'D)
> Your face is on every channel.

> ROB
> Once we make it to the border,
> we'll be okay.

> JAZZ
> I can't live like this, Robert! I <u>won't</u>
> live like this...

Rob grabs Jazz by the shoulders.

> ROB
> Do you love me?

Rob waits for an answer.

> ROB (CONT'D)
> Do you?

> JAZZ
> Yes. I love you.

> ROB
> Then trust me.

EXT. VISITOR CENTER, SHIES LODGE - NIGHT

Rob steals a silver Nissan Frontier in the parking lot.

INT. ROB'S FRONTIER - NIGHT

Rob speeds down a back road and loses the helicopter in the sky. Heads north. Through Washington State.

INT. AMERICAN AIRLINES - NIGHT

Thomas sits in the aisle seat, staring at a picture of Rob when he was a child.

INT. ROB'S FRONTIER - NIGHT

Rob pulls into a side road. Cuts off the headlights. Parks.

> ROB
> We should be safe here for the
> night.

EXT. TRUCK STOP - DAY

Thomas rushes from the rental car and gets inside with Ruby.

INT. RUBY'S CAR - CONTINUOUS

Ruby speeds away.

> RUBY
> He's heading to the border.

> THOMAS
> Whatever happens, John, don't let
> the cops get to him.

INT. ROB'S FRONTIER - DAY

Rob runs into a roadblock.

> ROB
> Fuck! Hang on...

Rob swerves around an idled car and pulls into a park called BLACK FALLS.

In the rear view mirror, an unmarked car follows Rob.

> JAZZ
> We have company.

>   ROB
>   (focusing on the
>   road)
>   How many?

>   JAZZ
>   Two.

Rob gains distance from the other cars, one an unmarked car and the other a cruiser.

EXT. WOODS, BLACK FALLS - DAY

Once Rob and Jazz reach the end of the road, they get out and make a run for it through the woods. They dash up a steep hill while the same unmarked car comes to a SCREECHING stop behind the truck.

Rob turns his shoulder, only to find a familiar face at a distance -- Detective Ruby! Then, out steps Thomas!

>   ROB
>   Go, Jazz! Run!

Rob and Jazz run through the lush woods.

About a half-mile in, the tip of Rob's shoe SNAGS on a swollen root protruding from the earth, resulting in a broken ankle. He falls to the ground, grabbing his ankle in agony. Jazz turns back around and tends to Rob.

>   JAZZ
>   (tugging at Rob)
>   Get up, Robert! Please!

>   ROB
>   Go! Go ahead! I'll catch up with
>   you!

He pulls out the other Beretta from his belt.

>   ROB (CONT'D)
>   (handing gun to
>   Jazz)
>   Here! Take it!

>   JAZZ
>   No! I can't do this without you,
>   Robert! Please! Get up!

> ROB
> Just go...I'll be right behind you...I
> promise...

> JAZZ
> I don't want to lose you...

Rob grabs Jazz by the face.

> ROB
> You're not going to lose me. I
> promise...

Jazz hugs Rob, grabs the Beretta, and takes off running. Rob hobbles to a tree to take cover as Ruby gains ground. Not too far from Ruby and Thomas are cops, and they have dogs.

> RUBY
> Rob! Make it easy on yourself!
> Give it up...

Rob pulls out the revolver and inserts the same bullet Ayker left him. He holsters the revolver behind his back.

Another quarter of a mile in, Rob stumbles across a river. He forces himself through the dense shrubbery and leaps into the raging water.

EXT. BLACK FALLS RIVER - CONTINUOUS

Ruby and Thomas cross the calmer side of the river while Rob lets his body go limp until the water gets rougher and choppier. He paddles across the river, grabs a tree branch, and pulls himself to the shore before the current sweeps him off a cliff!

> RUBY (O.S.)
> Robert, you have nowhere else to
> run!

Rob and Thomas hobble toward the waterfall while the detective approaches him with caution. The flap of his chocolate colored trench coat, once covering his holster, is flipped behind his back as if he's ready to draw.

> THOMAS
> (holding out his
> hands)
> Robert, listen to John. Please.
> Come back home with us...

Rob takes a couple of steps back and finds himself at the edge of the cliff. Looks below at the mouth of the waterfall. He turns his attention to the now grayish sky above. The police HELICOPTER closing in!

>   THOMAS (CONT'D)
>   ...It doesn't have to end this way.
>   Just come with us and we'll take
>   care of you!

>   ROB
>   Bullshit! I'm not going back to that
>   hellhole! I'd rather be dead!

>   RUBY
>   Rob, we can build a case against
>   these guys who shot Jimmy. We
>   can bring them down, together!
>   Listen to your father!

Rob takes one final glance at the waterfall.

>   THOMAS
>   Just think about what Jimmy would
>   want you to do!

>   ROB
>   You didn't know Jimmy. You
>   don't <u>know</u> me!

The detective hovers his right hand over the holster.

>   RUBY
>   Don't make me do it, Rob...

Rob looks down at his shadow darkening over the rocks below as the sun peeks through the gray clouds above. He tosses the Glock into the river, which sweeps the handgun into the waterfall. Ruby sighs. Relieved. He lowers his arms.

Then, Rob looks into the woods. Jazz is standing at a distance, her two pearl-shaped eyes peering directly at him.

>   ROB
>   I'm sorry, Jazz.

Rob reaches behind his back. Draws the revolver. Presses the barrel against his temple. Cocks the hammer...

THOMAS

Robert! No!

Ruby pulls his gun and SHOOTS Rob in the shoulder!

The gunshot spins Rob around like a top. He loses his bearings, balance, as well as the breath in his lungs, stumbles backward, and falls off the cliff!

Ruby runs to the edge of the cliff as Rob's lifeless body plummets through the waterfall.

EXT. PLUNGE POOL - CONTINUOUS

Rob plunges into the turbulent water, his eyes bolting open from the forceful impact. He tries to surface with his good arm, but the weight of the water bearing down on him is too much to handle. He uses both arms. Again, the pressure is too much for him...

Suddenly, James reaches his hand into the water!

Rob grabs James's hand, and James pulls Rob to the surface. Rob paddles his way to dry land without James. Just himself.

RUBY (O.S.)

Robert!

Rob hobbles along the shore, stands upright, and holds his gaze on Thomas. Then, as the helicopter descends, Rob takes off through the woods.

EXT. WOODS - CONTINUOUS

Jazz finds herself cornered by a swarm of cops.

Jazz keeps running, though, despite being outnumbered. Then, she gets tackled to the ground, cops pry the gun from her hand, and apprehend her.

EXT. BLACK FALLS - DAY

A group of cops places Jazz inside the back of the cruiser as Rob catches his breath against a tree and watches from afar.

INT. HOSTEL, MEXICO CITY - NIGHT

Nico rolls out of bed while a young, naked GIGOLO sleeps next to him. Nico puts on his pants. Walks to the half-broken mirror and splashes his disheveled face with dirty water.

Nico's phone rings. He checks the number. The name on the phone reads, "FOSTER." Nico turns to the gigolo who switches sleeping positions on the bed.

EXT. ALLEYWAY, MEXICO CITY - NIGHT

Nico exits from the back entrance of a seedy building where two LOCALS follow Nico.

He rounds a corner and loses the two locals. Spins around, only to find two more LOCALS blocking the path before him.

A BLACK VAN suddenly pulls in behind them!

The side door slides open. Nico backpedals, but, again, he's left with no room to escape.

INT. INTERNET CAFE - NIGHT

Rob scrolls through the NIGHTLY NEWS.

ON THE MONITOR

The headline: "AN AMERICAN KILLED BY MEXICAN DRUG CARTEL."
At the bottom of the page is a photo of Nico hanging upside down from a bridge, his intestines dangling from his abdomen.

INT. HOTEL ROOM, DUNES - NIGHT

Ruby flips on a light switch and checks out Rob's WALL OF SUSPECTS and VICTIMS. He examines each photo. Comes across a photo of Ayker. Removes the photo. Looks at it closely.

MONTAGE - THE AFTERMATH

-- EXT. AYKER'S HOUSE - DAY -- As news reporters wait outside, two FBI AGENTS haul Ayker's personal belongings, files and hard drives, from his house.

-- INT. SAN JORGE - DAY -- Two jail doors open. A mysterious black man steps forward into the dusty light.

-- INT. THE PLEASURESABER FACTORY - DAY -- The FEDS arrest each EMPLOYEE and seize pallets of COCAINE and HEROIN.

-- EXT. OLYMPIC PARK - DAY -- A swarm of FEDS arrest Officer Rodriquez while he plays with his two CHILDREN on the playground.

-- EXT. MALONE'S HOUSE - DAY -- The FEDS grab Malone while he's carrying groceries into his house.

-- EXT. SAN JORGE - DAY -- The inmate, Cedric Gaines, is escorted from prison, his family waiting to greet him.

-- INT. HOTEL ROOM - NIGHT -- Rob watches the NEWS REPORT about Cedric's release on TV.

INT./EXT. BJ'S PUB - NIGHT

A scar-faced Ayker downs the rest of his drink, pays the bartender, and then stumbles from the bar.

A snowy night, not a whiteout but, more or less, a dusting. Ayker holds out his tongue and tastes one of the powdery snow flakes. Bundles up. Drunkenly walks to car, swaying back and forth from the booze.

Ayker turns to a BLACK CAR in the parking lot. A shadowy man sits behind the steering wheel...

Right before Ayker steps into his beat-up Oldsmobile, he smells the air. Furrows his brows. Curious. Then, he shrugs off the oily stench in the cold air.

INT. AYKER'S OLDSMOBILE - NIGHT

As Ayker swerves over the yellow line, he rubs the blur from his eyes. He turns to the rear view mirror where he sees two headlights bearing down on him.

> AYKER
>> Asshole.

Suddenly, the engine shuts down. First, a CLUNK coming from the engine, then the car starts to sputter and smoke. The temperature gauge rises, forcing Ayker to pull the car over on the side of the road.

A car speeds around Ayker!

EXT. HIGHWAY - CONTINUOUS

Ayker pops the hood. Clears away the smoke and checks the engine. The coolant tank has been punctured. The tank is completely empty. He checks the oil. Empty as well.

> AYKER
>> (mumbling)
> Son of a bitch.

A car burning its high beams approaches Ayker from behind. Ayker shields his eyes from the bright headlights. A stranger dressed like the night steps out of the vehicle.

> STRANGER'S VOICE
>> (approaching Ayker)
> Car trouble?

> AYKER
> The damn thing just died on me.

Rob steps into the beam of headlights!

> AYKER (CONT'D)
>> (trembling)
> You?

Ayker inches his hand behind his back.

Suddenly, a Double Tap handgun shoots out from an updated contraption underneath Rob's sleeve, sleeker than before, faster than before, more fluid than before!

As Ayker grabs his gun, Rob shoots Ayker in the chest! Rob looms over Ayker's dying body. Rob finishes Ayker with a gunshot directly between the eyes!

EXT. TOPSIDE BEACH - DAY

Jazz and Phyllis swing Rob's two year old son, MOSES, who favors Rob more than Jazz, up and down along the sand. Jazz pauses in half-stride...

From a distance, Rob stands in a distant crowd, his long hair and black jacket blowing in the gusty ocean breeze.

> PHYLLIS (O.S.)
> Jasper? What's a matter?

Rob and Jazz lock eyes. They share a glance.

> PHYLLIS (CONT'D)
>> (louder)
> Jasper?

Jazz snaps from her trance.

> JAZZ
> Yeah.

> PHYLLIS
> What's wrong?

Jazz searches for Rob; however, he is lost in the crowd.

> JAZZ
> Nothing.

> PHYLLIS
> You sure?

> JAZZ
> Yes. I'm sure.

INT. ROB'S CONVERTIBLE CORVETTE - DAY

As Rob passes the sign to "Mexico" along the Pacific Coast Highway, he pulls out a cigarette from the glove box. Next to the pack lays the Double Tap on top of a photo of Anthony Foster with an X marked over his face.

Rob closes the glove box and hits "PLAY" on the stereo. The song "THE BOYS OF SUMMER" by Don Henley plays.

A ghost of a smile creeps onto the corner of Rob's face; and for a moment, Rob almost appears content with his life.

FADE TO BLACK.

www.ingramcontent.com/pod-product-compliance
Lightning Source LLC
Chambersburg PA
CBHW081147170626
46809CB00010B/3117